Wrong number . . . ?

We said good night and were heading toward the door when Anya's room phone started ringing. We paused, and Anya looked at us quizzically.

"That's odd," she said. "No one calls me on the hotel phone. . . ."

Joe and I exchanged glances. *Uh-oh.* "Let us hear it," he instructed as we all walked over to the phone.

Looking at us with fear in her eyes, Anya slowly picked up the receiver.

"Hello?"

"Anya." The voice on the other end of the line was seriously freaky—robotic, but deep and threatening. "You'd better attend those awards tomorrow night. If you don't, you might survive. But you'll never be able to live with yourself. Because the whole theater will be blown sky-high!"

THE HARDY BOYS

Undercover Brothers®

Available from Simon & Schuster

THE HARDY BOYS

Undercover Brothers®

BOYS

FRANKLIN W. DIXON

#39 Movie Mayhem

BOOK THREE IN THE DEATHSTALKER TRILOGY

Aladdin

New York   London   Toronto   Sydney   New Delhi

This book is a work of fiction. Any references to historical events, real people, or real locales are used fictitiously. Other names, characters, places, and incidents are the product of the author's imagination, and any resemblance to actual events or locales or persons, living or dead, is entirely coincidental.

ALADDIN
An imprint of Simon & Schuster Children's Publishing Division
1230 Avenue of the Americas, New York, NY 10020
First Aladdin paperback edition January 2012
Copyright © 2012 by Simon & Schuster, Inc.
All rights reserved, including the right of reproduction in whole
or in part in any form.
ALADDIN is a trademark of Simon & Schuster, Inc., and related logo
is a registered trademark of Simon & Schuster, Inc.
THE HARDY BOYS MYSTERY STORIES is a trademark of
Simon & Schuster, Inc.
HARDY BOYS UNDERCOVER BROTHERS and related logo are
registered trademarks of Simon & Schuster, Inc.
For information about special discounts for bulk purchases,
please contact Simon & Schuster Special Sales at 1-866-506-1949 or
business@simonandschuster.com.
The Simon & Schuster Speakers Bureau can bring authors to your live
event. For more information or to book an event, contact the
Simon & Schuster Speakers Bureau at 1-866-248-3049 or
visit our website at www.simonspeakers.com.
Designed by Karina Granda
The text of this book was set in Aldine 401 BT.
Manufactured in the United States of America 1211 OFF
10 9 8 7 6 5 4 3 2 1
Library of Congress Control Number 2011925433
ISBN 978-1-4424-0260-7
ISBN 978-1-4424-0261-4 (eBook)

TABLE OF CONTENTS

Missing

"Well, here we go again," I said with a sigh as my brother and I stood in the empty hotel suite. Empty, because the actress we'd spent the last week or so trying to protect, Anya Archer, was missing from her hotel room. On its own, this wouldn't be cause for alarm, but my bro and I had discovered that people would stop at nothing to get to Anya. They had set her trailer on fire, tried to electrocute her, and even stuffed a poisonous scorpion in her bag—and that's just for starters. Anya spent so much time in fear that she wasn't likely to go out on her own.

"We don't know for sure that anything's wrong yet," replied my brother, Frank, ever the logical one. "All we know is she's not here. Maybe she ran out for a coffee."

"Or maybe whoever's *really* been trying to scare the bejesus out of her hasn't been caught yet and took her," interrupted Zolo from behind us. Zolo, Anya's costar in the movie *Deathstalker* and a generally solid guy, had been the first to notice that Anya was missing when he'd stopped by her room for some pre-bedtime yoga. He'd alerted their movie director, Jaan, and . . . well, here we were.

See, a couple of weeks ago Frank and I got an assignment: protect Anya Archer from someone who was threatening her on the set of the movie *Deathstalker*. Deathstalker, for all of you uniniti-ated, is a pretty kick-butt comic series about a girl who gets special powers after an alien ship crashes into her house—including the power to sting like a scorpion. And yeah, I may have read an issue or two even before we got this assignment. The *Deathstalker* movie was one of the most hotly anticipated films in years—and actresses all over Hollywood had been dying for the part! But in a risky move, the director, Jaan St. John, had held a nationwide talent search and in the end decided to cast a total unknown—Anya Archer. Anya is seventeen and a total acting newbie. Her ace in the hole, though? She looks *exactly* like the Death-stalker from the comics.

But not everyone is psyched about Anya in the role. The Deathstalker blogs (yeah, there are blogs) are full of angry rants about how Anya's totally wrong for the part and is going to ruin the movie. Soon after shooting began, some seriously weird stuff went down. First someone set her trailer on fire. Then Anya got some scary texts, and flowers with threatening notes attached. When a creepy cut-up photo of her was left in her trailer, it became pretty clear the perpetrator had easy access to the set. Since Frank and I had arrived on the scene, things had gotten even more deadly. Someone electrified a microphone Anya was supposed to use at a fan convention. The shock was enough to fry her to death. Then someone messed with the safety net around a wind tunnel Anya was meant to use as part of a stunt, causing her stunt double to fall to a terrible death.

It wasn't like Frank and I had been sitting on our hands here. We'd identified not one, not two, but *three* culprits—one wacko fan, Myles Eccleston; one bodyguard who wanted to scare Anya into loving him, Big Bobby; and one production assistant—Anson—who had been blackmailed by Big Bobby into helping. Strangely enough, none of them had admitted to pulling the scariest acts, like the fire or the wind tunnel. Which meant we still had some unsolved crimes. And now Anya was missing.

Had she really just wandered off for a coffee, or was she in serious danger?

Just then, Jaan spoke into his phone. "I see. Thank you for your assistance, kind sir." He'd been on hold with the front desk, checking whether anyone had seen Anya leave. He looked up at Frank and me, his normally cheerful blue eyes looking serious. "It seems that no one downstairs saw our embattled leading lady leave."

Zolo sighed. "Look, as I said, she left her cell phone and wallet," he said, pointing at the coffee table. "Even if she was just headed for the Coffeebucks downstairs, I don't think she'd leave those behind."

"Maybe," Frank agreed in an even voice. "Or maybe she just grabbed some cash and ran. Maybe she didn't mean to be gone long."

Zolo's eyes flashed as he turned to face my brother. "You know, for her *boyfriend*, you don't seem very concerned."

I saw Frank's eyes pop. *Gulp.* Frank was posing as Anya's boyfriend on this mission; nobody besides Jaan knew that we were ATAC agents.

Unfortunately, Frank kept forgetting to act like he *loooooved* Anya. My brother isn't all that comfortable around the ladies, which made the whole charade even harder to keep up.

Frank cleared his throat. "No, I am very, *very* concerned. We'd better find Anya right away. Listen—" He looked at me. "Joe, why don't you stay here and search the room for more clues? Zolo and Jaan, you split up the remaining cast and crew and go from room to room, asking if anyone's seen Anya. I'll go downstairs and check the side and back exits. We'll find out if *anyone* saw Anya leave this hotel."

I nodded, giving my bro a little wink to let him know I was impressed. "Sounds like a plan." Zolo and Jaan eventually nodded too, and the three of them headed out into the hall.

With everyone gone, Anya's suite seemed kind of quiet—and kind of eerie. I shivered, hoping that nothing dangerous had happened. I decided to start with Anya's cell phone. Picking it up, I scrolled through all the recent calls and texts. There was a HEY, SIS, HOW'S THE MOVIE BIZ? text from her twelve-year-old little brother, Dan, to which she'd replied, MORE EXCITING THAN I IMAGINED . . . NOW DO YOUR MATH HOMEWORK!☺ There was also one voice mail, but when I listened to it, it was just her absentee Hollywood agent calling to "check in" an hour earlier. That didn't really tell me anything—even if Anya was still in her room at the time, she disliked her agent enough that she might have not answered his call.

I sighed and decided to move into the bedroom. Anya's huge king-size bed sat in the middle, pristinely made and totally untouched. On the right side was the closet and full-length mirror. I moved closer, noting that a few pairs of pants and tops were scattered on the rug. I frowned; had Anya's room been ransacked? Or was she just messy and indecisive about what to wear?

I walked around the bed and took note of something on the nightstand: a bouquet of creamy pink roses I hadn't noticed before. My heart sped up. Were they new? People had passed Anya flowers before—with threatening notes attached. Moving closer, I searched through the blooms for a card. But all I found was an empty envelope marked "Anya Archer" with her room number and today's date. So the flowers *were* new—but what had the card said? What had Anya done with it? I looked in the trash, and, finding nothing, got down on my hands and knees to look under the bed.

Just then I heard someone opening the door from the hall and sat up. "Hello?" I was hoping it would be Anya and we could all go to bed, secure in the knowledge that she was safe.

"I have returned," called Jaan from the sitting room. "Unfortunately, I haven't located our leading lady. Nobody I spoke with knew where she might be, not even Harmony, her most trusted confidante." He was referring to Harmony Caldwell, a pretty teen starlet who was playing Susie Q, Deathstalker's sidekick. She and Anya had gotten as close off-camera as their characters were on-camera. "She and her agent, Vivian, were watching a DVD. They said they'd actually invited Anya to join them, but she told them she'd be doing yoga with Zolo."

Jaan sighed as he entered the bedroom. "I'm becoming fearful," he said, and sank onto the bed. "This seems unlike Anya. She's usually so cautious. . . ." He sighed again, and he didn't have to finish for me to know where his thoughts were taking him. Anya wasn't the bravest of souls, and she'd made no secret of being freaked out by the threats. More than once, she'd threatened to leave the production if the culprit wasn't caught.

Would someone that afraid of being hurt just up and leave her hotel at night by herself?

I got up from the floor, nodding, and moved

into the bathroom, but nothing really looked out of place. Makeup was scattered all over the vanity, but from what I knew, that was pretty normal for girls. There was no threatening note scrawled on the mirror with lipstick. No "HELP ME, JOE!" notes scrawled on toilet paper with eyeliner pencil.

Suddenly I heard a pounding on the door, and then Jaan getting up to open it.

"Is it true?" I heard Stan Redmond, the no-nonsense producer of *Deathstalker*, bellow. "Zolo just came by my room babbling some nonsense about Anya being missing. Is it true?"

Jaan sighed. "It . . . well . . . her status is ambiguous right now."

"What does *that* mean?" Stan demanded. "Is she here or isn't she?"

"She is not," Jaan admitted, "but that doesn't mean she's missing, necessarily. She might have stepped out for some night air. . . ."

Stan made a sound at that point that I couldn't quite identify—the closest I could come would be "angry raspberries." "Left on her own? What if something happens to her? That's just what we need. This production is running off the rails, and the tabloids are going nuts with the accidents we've had. We need something good to happen,

Jaan—and fast. We need some *good* press."

Jaan sounded a little taken aback. "I'd be satisfied with our intrepid heroine coming back, safe and sound."

Stan sighed loudly. "Anya! I told you not to hire her, Jaan. I told you she wasn't up for the task. She's an amateur, plain and simple." I heard them walk back to the bedroom, and the mattress sighing as Stan plopped himself down. "I'd say we were lucky she didn't get scared off by all this craziness, but maybe we weren't so lucky. Maybe we would have been luckier if she *had* been scared off and we had ended up hiring a *real* actress, like that Amy Alvaro."

I swallowed. Maybe Stan was just letting off a little steam, but—did he just say he wished things like the wind tunnel accident and the fire *had* scared off Anya? Frank and I had wondered for a while whether Stan would have preferred a "name" actress in the Deathstalker part. It would definitely help the movie's chances at the box office—and producers are all about the bottom line.

On a whim, I typed out a quick text to headquarters to get an updated suspect profile on Stan. HQ texted back a few minutes later.

SUSPECT PROFILE

Name: Stan Redmond

Hometown: Pacific Palisades, California

Physical description: Age 61, 5'9", 170 pounds. Thinning gray hair, brown eyes, droopy jowls.

Occupation: Successful film producer

Suspicious behavior: Wishing that Anya had been scared off by threatening texts, pranks, etc., allowing him to cast a "name" actress.

Suspected of: Trying to cast a big-name actress as Deathstalker after scaring Anya out of the role.

Possible motive: Guaranteeing the film's box-office success.

Hmmm. Nothing we didn't already know, unfortunately. Almost immediately, my phone beeped again—another text, this one from Zolo.

STILL ?ING AROUND, BUT VANCE IS MISSING 2 AND NO 1 KNOWS WHERE HE IS.

I blinked at the screen. Vance Bainbridge was the vain and kind of dimwitted actor who played

Deathstalker's love interest—a role created for this movie. And now *he* was missing too?

Vance going out alone would not be as weird as Anya leaving the hotel by herself. He had nothing to fear by leaving—but it *did* seem a little strange that no one knew where he'd gone. And just the day before, Frank and I had seen him and his girlfriend, Amy Alvaro, chatting gleefully about how the Deathstalker role would soon be Amy's. They made no secret of the fact that they thought the movie would be better off with Amy in the lead role. So had Vance finally decided to take matters into his own hands?

I typed off another text to headquarters.

SUSPECT PROFILE

Name: Vance Bainbridge

Hometown: Los Angeles, California

Physical description: Age 19, 6'2", 190 pounds. Blond hair, hazel eyes. Voted hottest teen actor three years in a row at the Big Apple Awards.

Occupation: Actor; has appeared in nine major motion pictures since making his Hollywood debut at the age of thirteen.

Suspicious behavior: Talking with his girlfriend Amy Alvaro about being sure she could take over

Deathstalker part within days; disappearing the same night as Anya.

Suspected of: Kidnapping or harming Anya.

Possible motive: Getting his girlfriend the part of Deathstalker.

Staring at my smartphone moments later, I sighed, wishing that headquarters had given me some better information—or that I had found some better clues. Even if Vance was somehow involved, I still had no idea whether Anya had left on her own, or whether she'd been taken forcibly. I decided to check the sitting room again. Maybe there was something I'd missed.

With a quick nod at Stan and Jaan, who were still arguing about Anya, I walked through the bedroom and toward the sitting room. But at the threshold to the sitting room, I froze at the sound of a familiar voice coming from the couch just out of view.

Smarmy. Arrogant. *Vance!*

"I think this has gone a little too far. Now she's going to get what she deserves!"

Secrets

I plowed through the door to Anya's suite and ran over to the TV in the sitting room, flipping it on as quickly as I could. Sure enough, the cheesy music theme from *Hollywood Secrets Live* played as the show came back from a commercial. I hadn't missed anything!

On-screen, a brunette anchorwoman beamed into the camera. "And now for the story we told you about before the commercial. What secrets are being kept on the *Deathstalker* set?"

I hopped a little in anticipation. All my questioning downstairs had led to dead ends—nobody had seen Anya leave the hotel, not through side entrances, back entrances, or even the entrance to the kitchen. The kitchen employees, though, had been watching a trashy little gem of a show called *Hollywood Secrets Live*. Before the show cut to a commercial, it had teased a story that promised "new revelations about the *Deathstalker* cast" while showing footage of Anya at the fan convention.

The show now cut to footage from an old Vance Bainbridge movie, *Serious Hail*. On-screen, Vance sneered at an offscreen victim: "I think this has gone a little too far. Now she's going to get what she deserves!"

"Aaack!"

The sound was barely audible, but I know my brother's freaked-out noises better than anyone. "Joe? Is that you?"

Looking a little sheepish, Joe peered around the doorway into the living room. "Frank? Is that the TV?"

I nodded. "Sorry, did I scare you?"

He shrugged.

"Is anyone else here?" I asked. "Bring everyone in. This show is doing some story about behind-the-scenes *Deathstalker* secrets."

Joe called behind him and moved into the room, followed by Jaan and Stan.

"What's going on?" Stan asked gruffly. "I've just heard about Anya. . . ."

I held a finger to my lips and gestured to the television. "Big secret about the *Deathstalker* cast coming up!"

Now the brunette announcer was back. "What secret is Hollywood bad boy Vance keeping from his girlfriend, Amy Alvaro?" Then they cut to grainy footage of Vance at a dark lounge—and we all let out huge gasps.

Vance was cuddling with Anya!

"This footage, captured just an hour ago, proves that Vance has gotten awfully close to his *Deathstalker* leading lady, Anya Archer. While on-set rumors had them fighting early in the shoot, clearly Vance has been stung by his costar's love!"

The show then moved on to some sitcom star going into rehab as my bro and I turned to each other in disbelief.

"Did you see that?" asked Joe.

I nodded. "They were watching this in the kitchen downstairs. No one there saw Anya leave, by the way."

Joe let out his breath in a low whistle. "Well, at least now we know where she went—and who she went with. That was a secret, all right. I don't think anybody in this room knew!"

I glanced at Jaan and Stan.

"Most certainly not," agreed Jaan, looking

stunned and a little amused. "I didn't realize that romance was blooming right under my nose!"

Stan coughed and shook his head. "That's definitely a shocker," he said. "Sure to be on the covers of all the tabloids." He glanced at Frank. "Don't take it too hard, kid. Anya's just like everyone else in the world and can't resist a pretty face."

Jaan held up his hands, as if to say, *Enough*. "What matters is that my leading lady is not in harm's way," he said with a smile.

"Right," Stan agreed with a nod. "And it means we can resume production tomorrow, and not incur a costly delay, which is what I care about. That and Anya's safety, of course."

Of course. I crooked an eyebrow in Joe's direction. Stan was a gruff guy . . . but was he a little *too* gruff when it came to Anya?

Just then we all heard footsteps rushing from the elevator to Anya's room, and Zolo burst in, looking seriously keyed up.

"Okay," he said to Joe, not waiting for anyone to acknowledge him. "You got my text?"

Joe nodded. "Actually, I—"

But Zolo wouldn't wait for him to finish. "So Vance is missing, you know that much. Buzz said he didn't know anything about Anya leaving the hotel, but he does know that she drinks coffee, so maybe that has something to do with it. Jimbo, you know Jimbo, the new Scorch, *he* said that he hasn't seen Anya since yesterday, but he did notice that she doesn't eat much at craft services, so he thought maybe she got hungry and went for a bite to eat. He says there's this great Vietnamese place two blocks from here, by the way. And Kelly from wardrobe, *she* said—"

Looking impatient, Stan walked over and clapped Zolo on the shoulder. "Calm down, kid. Turns out she's fine."

Zolo looked confused. "She is?" he asked. "Then where is she?"

Just then the elevator in the hallway dinged and we could hear loud giggling in the hallway. Within seconds, Vance and Anya walked into the suite—or maybe I should say *Bizarro Vance and Anya*, because they both looked a little—well—off. Vance was wearing what looked like a curly black wig, and he had a skinny black mustache perched somewhat crookedly over his lip. Anya was wearing a long red wig, sunglasses, and a baggy trench coat. When the two of them finally looked up from each other and saw the collection of people gathered in the sitting room, they gasped—then giggled even harder.

"Oh—hi!" Anya greeted us between giggles.

"What are you all doing here? Did something happen?"

Zolo scoffed. "Did something happen," he muttered under his breath, shaking his head.

Stan moved toward the couple. "Listen," he said gruffly. "You kids better not disappear without telling anyone where you're going ever again, you got that?" Anya nodded obediently, as Stan turned to Vance and gave him a nod. "Good night, everyone." With that, he turned on his heel and left the room.

Jaan cleared his throat, bringing all eyes to him. "My beloved thespians?" he said, looking expectantly at his star actors. "Is there anything you two would like to tell me?"

Anya looked hesitant, but Vance immediately broke into a proud, almost goofy smile, then ripped off the curly black wig. "Yes!" he cried, throwing his arm around Anya. "Anya and I are in love!" And with that, he leaned over and gave Anya a noisy smooch.

Joe moved closer to me and gave me a perplexed look. "Awkward much?" he whispered, as Vance continued to kiss his new sweetheart.

I nodded. "They're not shy, huh?" I whispered back.

Joe cleared his throat, and we all fumbled

around awkwardly, not knowing what to do with ourselves, but Vance's enthusiastic PDA continued. "What about Amy?" Joe asked finally, and Vance broke off, looking stricken, as Anya pulled off her wig and struggled to collect herself.

"Well . . ." Vance shrugged, looking past us. "It's very unfortunate that our relationship will have to end, but . . . the heart wants what the heart wants. . . ."

"*Will* have to?" Joe echoed, looking even more surprised. "She doesn't know yet?"

Suddenly Zolo, who'd been standing open-mouthed, seemed to shake off his shock and come to life. "What about *Frank*?" he asked, looking disgusted and a little dubious.

Frank? Frank! Oh, shoot!

I'd momentarily forgotten that no one besides Anya and Jaan knew who Joe and I really were. They thought Joe was an extra and that I was Anya's boyfriend from back home. In fact, Zolo had gotten in the somewhat weird habit of calling me "Boyfriend Frank."

"Oh . . . yeah!" I cried. I was trying to look appropriately horrified and betrayed, but from Joe's reaction, I had a feeling that I looked more like I'd eaten a bad burrito. "How could you . . . um . . . ?"

Before I could finish, Zolo suddenly threw up his hands and stormed out of the room. "Crazy set," I thought I heard him mutter as he stomped off. "Commercials are never this nuts. . . ."

I swallowed hard and looked at my brother. *Oops.* But Joe wasn't looking at me—he was staring at Vance, who I now realized was giving me his "sincerest of sincere" looks. I recognized it from his work on the movie. It kind of made *him* look like he'd had a bad burrito.

"Listen, Frank," he said. "Sometimes love isn't pretty. I'm so sorry for stealing your girl."

I looked at him, not sure what to do. *Why couldn't Joe have played the boyfriend role?* "That's . . . okay, Vance."

Vance nodded, like I'd made the right decision. "It's probably better this way. If she'd truly loved you, I couldn't have stolen her away."

Was he insulting me? "Um . . . right."

"Listen," Jaan announced, looking like this conversation was starting to tire him out. "It's late. We have an early call time tomorrow. Let's all go to bed, and we can discuss this in the morning."

Anya nodded. "That sounds like a good idea," she said eagerly. I wasn't sure whether she was eager to sleep, or just eager to get rid of all of us.

"Good night, my Sweet Rose," Vance said in a

honeyed voice, then leaned in to give her another uncomfortably long kiss. Joe gave me an amazed look, and then cleared his throat again. But it was a few seconds before Vance came up for air. "Sweet dreams. I know I'll be dreaming of you tonight." With a gentle pat on her head, Vance nodded at the rest of us and left the room. Jaan looked from my brother and me to Anya, shook his head, and said simply, "Good night," before following Vance out the door.

In the silence that followed, Joe and I looked at Anya eagerly. I think we both expected her to burst out with an explanation, but instead she stared doggedly at an invisible spot on the rug, twirling a lock of black hair around her finger.

"Really?" Joe burst out finally, shattering the silence. *"Vance?"*

Anya sighed. *"I'm-so-sorry,"* she blurted. "I should have told you. It's just . . . it happened so fast!"

"Did he show up this evening?" Joe asked. "With a bunch of roses?"

Anya nodded. "He said . . . he couldn't stop thinking about me. My eyes. My lips. The way I smiled at him as Deathstalker." She paused. "The card with the roses said. 'I want you to be my leading lady in real life.'" She smiled, then immediately blushed crimson.

"He doesn't seem like your type," I pointed out.

Anya looked up at me. "Oh, Frank," she said with a sigh. "I'm sorry. I realize I put you in a weird position with . . . with everyone thinking you're my boyfriend. And the truth is, I never would have thought Vance was my type either. But he showed up here tonight saying all these beautiful things and with these crazy disguises. He said he wanted to sneak out of the hotel and take me out for the night." She smiled. "It sounds so silly, but it was so much fun. I had *fun* with Vance tonight. He may not be the deepest guy. But he's . . ." She trailed off.

"Built?" Joe supplied, not quite hiding his disgust.

Anya shook her head. "Sweet," she finished. "I'm sorry, guys. I never meant to scare you, and next time, I'll tell you where I'm going. But after everything that's happened . . . it was nice to get away from all that and have a good time."

I looked at Joe, and he nodded. *After everything that's happened.* I knew that my brother and I were both thinking about how we had caught Big Bobby and Anson earlier that day—but that they hadn't confessed to some of the scariest stuff. It was clear that Anya hoped everything was over, but that was far from certain.

Just then Anya's phone beeped—it was her text message signal. She ran over to her phone. "Oh, that's probably Vance. We left so quickly earlier, I left my phone and my wallet sitting here. Luckily, he paid for everything." She smiled. "He said it was more romantic that way."

She looked so happy I wondered if she had ever had a guy treat her to a night out before.

But when she grabbed her phone and looked down, her face turned pale. "Oh my—oh no," she whispered. I ran over to grab the phone out of her hand and looked down at the screen.

YOU MADE A BIG MISTAKE TONIGHT. AT THE BIG APPLE AWARDS, YOU'LL BE WITH VANCE FOR THE LAST TIME!

Feel the Anger

"**A**nother day, another chance for this wacko to make a crazy threat," I said with a sigh as Frank and I walked to the set the next morning. The cast had left Central Park for the day and was shooting near a subway station in Brooklyn. As we passed the security gate, I looked at the crew milling around, ready to get to work. To look at the scene, you'd never know how much craziness this production had already seen, or how freaked out its leading lady was. We'd had to spend a long time reassuring Anya before she felt comfortable letting us leave her room the previous night. The text she'd been sent had come from a disposable cell phone and was untraceable . . . just like all the others.

"Don't be so negative," Frank chided. "You could say, another day, another chance for us to catch the creep."

I sighed again. "I could," I agreed. "I guess this case is just kind of getting to me. We keep thinking we've caught the guy, and another creep pops up out of the woodwork."

"We'll find him," Frank insisted, looking confident. "You'll see." He looked across the street to the subway entrance, past the security line. "Hey! Isn't that Dalton?"

I followed his gaze. Sure enough, propped up on crutches and with a huge cast on one leg stood Dalton Friedrich, Deathstalker blogger extraordinaire. We hadn't seen Dalton since an accident had sent him tumbling off a roof near the start of our case. Another Deathstalker fan had set him up, basically, trying to embarrass him. But there he was, arguing with a security guard, no doubt trying to plead his case to get on set.

"Hey," I called, as Frank and I walked over. "Dalton! How are you recovering?"

Dalton looked up at us. "Oh, hey," he said, looking a little disappointed. I wondered if he was hoping to see one of the actors, particularly Anya, on whom he had a huge crush. Dalton was a mega fan of the Deathstalker comics, and he'd become the most prominent blogger about the *Deathstalker* movie. "I'm starting to do a little better. It's been a painful recovery." He sighed dramatically, flashing a glance at the security guard. "Which is why I thought Anya might be willing to see me. I know security is tight on the set, but she must know all about the . . . incident at FanCon and what I went through?"

Frank shook his head. "I don't think Anya's seeing much of anybody right now, bro," he told Dalton. "Security *is* pretty tight."

Dalton's face fell. "Is this because of her *thing* with Vance Bainbridge?"

"You know about that?" I asked, and then immediately thought, *Of course he does*. Dalton knew everything there was to know about the *Deathstalker* movie. I wouldn't be surprised if he knew about the Vance thing before it even aired on *Hollywood Secrets Live*. He definitely had his ear to the ground, especially when it came to Anya.

Dalton turned to me. "Everyone knows about it," he said scornfully. "I can't believe Anya's wasting her time with that Hollywood jerk. He's so bland and boring. A waste of space."

I glanced at Frank: *Harsh much?* But given Dalton's feelings for Anya, along with the fact that most of the blogosphere was holding a grudge against Vance for being cast in the made-up role of Deathstalker's love interest, his tone wasn't all that surprising.

Frank shrugged. "He must have some good qualities," he pointed out, "if Anya's fallen for him, right?"

Dalton snorted. "Puh-*leeze!*" he said, rolling his eyes. "That guy is like an animated Ken doll—no personality at all. I just can't believe their romance is real. It seems like a career move to me."

I crooked an eyebrow. "A career move?" I asked. "For Anya or for Vance?"

Dalton shrugged. "Both? Who knows?" he asked, digging in his messenger bag and pulling out a sheaf of tabloids, all of which seemed to feature a story on the *Deathstalker* movie. "All I know is, you can bet they'll be on the cover of every one of these magazines this week. And that's the kind of publicity money can't buy. Their so-called 'relationship' will make them more famous than either one of them could have gotten on their own. I have to believe that's why she's putting up with him."

Just then I heard a commotion coming from one of the trailers closest to the station.

"Who needs you?" a strident female voice demanded. "Good-for-nothing . . . selfish . . ."

Frank looked at me. "That's Vance's trailer, isn't it?"

I gulped and turned to Dalton. "Uh, gotta go."

Without another word, Frank and I ran over to the trailer where all the noise was coming from. We were just in time to see the metal door bang open and the beautiful—but furious—Amy Alvaro storm down the tiny stairs.

"I can't *believe* this!" she screamed as Vance appeared in the doorway, looking chastened. "For her? *Her?* That *child?* She's not even a good actress!"

Vance looked like he was about to say something, but he bit his lip and hung his head instead. "I'm sorry," he said quietly.

Amy glared at him. "You sure are," she agreed, then turned and glared at Frank and me, who were standing in her way. "*Excuse* me," she huffed, pushing Frank to the side as she stomped past us.

I turned to watch her stalk off set, a blaze of dark hair and anger, before turning back to Vance, who was staring at a spot on his shoes, looking sheepish. "You just *now* told her about you and Anya?" I asked.

Vance sighed. "Well . . . yes," he admitted. "I wanted to tell her earlier, before the pictures got out. But Amy was doing a shoot for *Elle* in Montauk last night, and I didn't realize Anya and I were being followed."

Frank looked as incredulous as I felt. "You must feel awful," he said, looking from Vance to the spot where Amy had disappeared and back again.

Vance shrugged, and a light seemed to go out in his eyes. "The heart wants . . ."

". . . what it wants," I finished, remembering that he'd said the same thing last night.

Vance nodded, looking a little embarrassed. "Right," he said, sighing and running a hand through his fluffy blond hair. "Well, they need me on the set."

"We were just headed there," Frank said.

Vance looked less than thrilled to hear that, but he was quiet as he set out for the subway entrance ahead of us. Frank and I followed in silence.

The scene being filmed this morning was an argument between Vance's character, Parker, and Zolo's character, an alien named Asp. It took place on a subway platform that the movie producers had paid the city to shut down for a few hours. In the scene, Parker mistakenly thinks that Asp is hurting Sissy Stiles, when in fact the alien was helping her recover from an injury she'd gotten as Deathstalker. Anya and Zolo were already made up and on the set. As soon as we got down the stairs to the platform, Vance ran over to Anya and gave her a huge, wet kiss.

"I missed you, Dumpling!" he cooed in a whispery voice.

I couldn't keep the disgust from showing on my face as I caught Frank's eye.

Dumpling? he mouthed, looking just as disturbed as I felt.

The only person on the set who looked even more weirded out than Frank or me was Zolo. He stood behind Anya and Vance in his full Asp regalia, looking as though he'd just tasted something putrid. Finally he shook his head and looked away, rubbing his temples like the scene was giving him a headache.

I leaned over and whispered to Frank, "What do you think about what Dalton said? About Vance dating Anya for his career?"

Frank shrugged. "I wouldn't put it past him," he whispered back. "But that breakup with Amy looked serious. He seems to really care about her; I can't see him doing that just for his career."

I nodded slowly. "True," I said, "but let's keep an eye on it."

Just then Jaan strode over, holding a copy of the script. "Attention, my little artistes," he began, gesturing for Vance and Anya to cool it down. "I hate to put a halt to your expression of young love, but Vance, you're tardy, which means we're behind schedule."

"Sorry, Jaan," said Vance, not meeting the director's eye. "I had . . . personal business to clear up."

Jaan nodded. "Accepted. But in the future, please clear up your business before your call time. Now, let's invest ourselves in the scene. As you know, this is a huge misunderstanding between Asp and Parker. Both of your characters are very distressed because you both care so much about Sissy. Understand?"

"I got it," Zolo said shortly, making abrupt little motions like a boxer warming up for a fight. "Let's do this."

Jaan held up his hand to hold Zolo off. "Now, to make the scene as authentic as possible, I want you both to remember a time in your lives when you were incensed. Can you do that? I'm talking about a time you would have breathed fire if you could. A time when you were so outraged that you felt like you might combust."

Vance looked thoughtful, as though he were trying to choose just such a memory, but Zolo looked—actually—really furious. "Got it," Zolo cut in again. "I'm ready. Let's shoot."

But Vance looked perplexed. "I'm torn, Jaan," he

said, holding a finger to his chin. "There was one time I was left off the nomination list for a SAG award, despite turning in really exceptional work. That had me pretty angry. But I'm also remembering a time when I was a child and was promised dessert if I ate my veggies, but my mother didn't specify *how many* veggies, so I suffered through two brussels sprouts and *still* didn't get dessert. What I felt then was a very different, more primal anger. Perhaps that's more appropriate?"

Jaan looked confused. "Ahem . . . how did you proceed in each case?"

Vance looked satisfied, remembering. "I did *not* attend the SAG Awards that year. Oh, and in the other case, I knocked my plate off the table and stormed off to my room."

Jaan nodded. "Well then, that's your clear inspiration. The brussels sprouts memory."

Behind Vance, Zolo seemed to be getting more impatient with every word. As soon as Jaan chose a memory for Vance, he broke in. "All right. Let's go. I'm ready."

But Vance turned to Zolo like they had all the time in the world. "What's your memory?"

Zolo glared at him. "What?"

"I think your colleague is asking what memory of outrage you're going to draw from," Jaan broke in. "I want you to pull your anger from a very raw place. *Feel* the anger, like it's happening to you right now."

Zolo's glare intensified and settled on Jaan. "Done," he said. "I'm ready. Can we just start?"

Vance held up a finger. "If I may, Zolo, I think you're being hasty about this. Jaan is trying to help."

Zolo took a deep breath, but when he spoke, he still looked furious. "I am telling you," he said between clenched teeth, turning to Jaan. "I am *ready* to feel the anger. Okay?"

Jaan looked at Zolo, suddenly seeming to grasp the anger coming off him in waves. "Very well," he said. "Quiet on the set! We're about to shoot."

Frank and I moved off to the sides as the camera and lighting people got into place. Vance and Zolo got on their marks, Zolo breathing slowly through his nose, as though he was trying to calm himself down.

Finally Jaan yelled "Action!" and the scene began.

"I want you to get away from her!" Vance shouted, and I had to admit that Jaan's technique seemed very effective. He sounded livid. "She's my girlfriend, and if you hurt her, I'll kick your alien butt."

Zolo took in a breath, his eyes smoldering,

and then suddenly erupted into a furious scream. "She's not your *PROPERTY!*" he shouted, practically blowing the roof off the subway station. "I'm trying to PROTECT her! You moron!"

Suddenly Jaan leaped up. "Cut!" he called, running up from his director's chair to approach Vance and Zolo. "My dear Zolo, I think you're perhaps a little *too* angry, too soon. You need to give the tension time to build. Understood?"

But Zolo wasn't even looking at him. His eyes were glued to Vance, burning with anger. "Sure. Okay," he said flatly.

Jaan looked a little hesitant, but he nodded. "Very well."

The director took his seat, and the scene began again. Again, Zolo's anger seemed to dominate the conversation, burning into an intense fury before Vance could get out more than one of his lines. I frowned at Frank, wondering what was going on with the usually mellow actor. Was Zolo just having a tough day? Or had something happened to *make* him this angry?

Twice more, Jaan cut the scene and tried to calm Zolo down. But both times, the next take was just as bad. Behind the boys, Anya stood on her mark, looking a little more perplexed each time Jaan yelled, "Cut!"

"Zolo?" she asked after the third take. "Are you okay?"

Zolo bit his lip.

Before he could reply, Vance moved closer to him. "My man," Vance began, a little too chummily. "Back when I worked on *Radioactive Worms 2*, the director gave me a stellar piece of advice. And that advice was: Just be."

Zolo looked up at Vance, confused, but Vance just nodded in a satisfied way.

"What?" asked Zolo.

"Just be," Vance repeated, continuing to nod. "You need to feel the part deep down in your soul, and just *do it*, man. Right, Anya?"

Anya looked confused, but she nodded. "Okay, Vance."

Zolo glared at Vance again, gritting his teeth. "Okay. I'm ready, Jaan. Let's shoot."

Jaan looked a little dubious, but he called for everyone to take their places, and then yelled, "Action!"

"I want you to get away from her!" Vance shouted for the fourth time, his inflection, amazingly enough, identical to the previous three times. The brussels sprouts memory really seemed to be working for him. "She's my girlfriend, and—*aaaagh!*"

Without warning, Zolo suddenly sprang forward from his mark *and punched Vance in the face!*

Stunned, Vance reeled back, grabbing his jaw, but quickly recovered and returned the blow. Zolo was ready, though, knocking Vance's fist aside and shoving him forward—toward the subway tracks!

"Halt!" Jaan cried, leaping up from his chair. "Stop it this instant, you ruffians! This isn't in the script!"

But Zolo was like a man possessed. He rained punches down on Vance, as Vance seemed to recover a bit and start to fight back. The station was filled with the sickening sound of fists hitting muscle, amplified by the microphones both actors were wearing. Zolo stepped away for a second, glaring down at Vance, and everyone went quiet, thinking he was about to stop. But then Zolo glanced back at Anya and shoved Vance down onto the subway tracks, jumping in after him!

Chaos seemed to break out. Everyone started yelling, moving toward the fighting actors as the punching sounds started up again. Jimbo, the young special effects guy who had replaced his injured boss, Scorch, suddenly came running into the frame, his shouts rising above the insanity.

"Stop it!" he screamed. "*Stop it right now!* The third rail is live—and if you guys hit it, you're going to get shocked with a thousand volts of electricity!"

Only One Reason

Joe and I jumped into action, jetting toward the subway tracks. See, in most cities, subways are powered by electricity. If you look at subway tracks, there are three rails—two for the wheels of the train to run on, and a third rail that gives the train power to run. Trains have a little metal piece or "foot" that juts out and rides along the third rail, bringing power to the train. But that means when there's no train on the tracks, that third rail is still filled with deadly electricity—enough to fry anyone foolish or unlucky enough to touch it.

Which made what Zolo and Vance were doing *extremely* dangerous.

Joe and I ran down the platform and swung

ourselves down into the depressed tracks, where Zolo and Vance were still brawling.

"You bigheaded moron!" Zolo was shouting, aiming another punch at Vance. "You think you can have anything you want! I'm tired of it!"

Vance dodged the blow and looked at Zolo in disbelief. "What's gotten into you, dude?" he asked, raising a hand to block and then trying to wrap an arm around Zolo's neck. "Don't make me hurt you! I'm an excellent wrestler!"

"Hey, break it up, break it up," Joe shouted, as the two of us moved closer. Joe seamlessly slipped behind Zolo and grabbed him around the shoulders, while I grabbed Vance around the waist. Together, we pulled them closer to the platform—away from the third rail.

"Calm down, guys," I said in what I hoped was a soothing voice, as I struggled to restrain Vance, who still lunged at Zolo. "Whatever this is about, it's not worth it. It's not worth your lives. Let's get back to the platform."

"Yeah," agreed Vance, taking a deep breath and glaring at his costar. "Psycho," he added under his breath.

Zolo sighed and looked away, but he followed Joe, Vance, and me as we climbed back up to the platform. Jaan was standing there, waiting.

"What on earth has gotten into you?" he asked Zolo incredulously. His eyes flashed. "I should dismiss you for that! That was unprofessional, not to mention incredibly perilous! Why would you behave that way?"

Zolo pulled his mouth tight and looked down at the floor. He didn't look sorry, exactly—but he did look upset. "Sorry Jaan," he muttered finally.

"Sorry?" Jaan asked. "Is that your only response? Zolo, what has gotten into you?" he repeated.

Zolo shook his head. His eyes moved briefly to Anya, who was watching the scene openmouthed, and then back to the floor. "Just having a bad day," he muttered, so quietly I could barely hear him.

Jaan stared at him for a few seconds, clearly not knowing what to think, then he glanced at Joe and me. I shrugged. I had no idea what had gotten into the normally calm Zolo. He did yoga, for crying out loud!

Jaan turned to Vance. "Are you harmed, my boy?" he asked, his voice warming a bit.

Vance glared at Zolo again and shrugged. "No permanent harm done," he said. "Although I would like an apology."

Zolo continued to stare at the floor. "Sorry," he mumbled.

Jaan cleared his throat.

"Very well," he said, taking a deep breath. "Zolo, I remain befuddled as to what your problem is today. But since this is unlike you, I'm going to give us all a chance to recover our senses. Let's take five. Everyone relax for a few minutes and then we'll proceed with the scene."

There was a moment of quiet, and then everyone took off in different directions, with Vance running over to Anya and embracing her like a dying man given one last reprieve. I mouthed, *Following Zolo* to Joe and then fell into step behind the grumpy actor.

"Hey, Zolo," I said. "Mind if I join you?"

Zolo glanced up at me as if seeing me for the first time and shrugged. "Whatever."

We walked upstairs and into the blinding sun. Zolo's trailer was the third from the station, next to Anya's and Vance's. He walked in without a word, nearly closing the door in my face, but I grabbed it. What was *with* Zolo today?

I thought about what Joe and I had talked about the night before, just before going to bed. Zolo was a smart guy; he'd clearly noticed that my "romance" with Anya was a little weird, and he was just as concerned about her safety as anyone. Before he figured out who we really were on his own, we'd decided to break our cover to him.

"Hey, Zolo," I said, as he grabbed a soda out of the mini-fridge and settled down on a couch. "I have a confession to make."

Zolo looked up at me, a surprising glint of anger in his eyes. "What, that you're not really Anya's boyfriend?" he asked. "That you were hired to protect her from the weird threats and attacks?"

My mouth dropped open. "I, uh—how did you know?" I asked. Was he a mind reader?

But Zolo just shrugged and took a sip of his soda. "I'm not a moron like Vance or half the pretty boys in this industry. I can put two and two together. You and your brother are always around after something happens to Anya, and she doesn't really seem that into you. No offense."

"None taken," I replied, impressed. I knew Zolo was a smart guy, but I'd never expected him to figure out our real role on his own. What else had he figured out? "Listen, Zolo—what's wrong with you, man? I've never seen you this . . . angry."

Zolo looked up at me out of the corner of his eye, as if debating whether to say something. Then he closed his eyes and took another sip of his soda. When his eyes opened again, his expression was blank. "Nothing's going on with me," he said in a monotone. "Just having a bad day."

"Come on," I insisted, leaning closer. "*Some-*

thing must be getting to you for you to attack Vance like that."

A rueful smile crossed his face. "It's been a wild couple of days," he said, shrugging and hiding behind his soda can again. "There's a lot of stress on the set, all this weird stuff happening. Plus, I've never liked Vance."

I frowned; okay, he had a point there. Vance didn't have a lot of friends on set, and he and Zolo had never been close. I could see them arguing; I could see Zolo making a sarcastic comment. But why would he *attack* Vance—putting both of them at huge risk in the process?

Just then I heard a phone ringing. Zolo didn't move, but I looked around and saw that the ring was coming from a backpack sitting on the dining table.

"You gonna get that?" I asked Zolo.

He put down the soda can, and all at once I noticed a look of panic on his face. What was up?

"Zolo?" I pressed.

Zolo shook his head, looking away. "Ah, no . . . You know . . . it's probably a telemarketer. . . ."

I frowned. On a cell phone? Unlikely.

"How about I get it for you?" I asked, striding over and grabbing the backpack before Zolo could refuse. I unzipped the zipper, dug my hand in, and pulled out the phone just as it rang for the last time.

When I looked down, my stomach clenched.

It was a disposable cell phone!

"Who was it?" Zolo asked brightly. "Nobody, right? Probably a telemarketer. See, I've been getting these calls. . . ."

"Why do you have a disposable cell phone?" I asked, cutting him off and holding up the cheap plastic phone. Disposable cell phones probably had some totally well-meaning users, but all the people I'd ever seen with them had them for only one reason: to avoid being traced. Meaning that they could make all the threatening calls—or texts—they wanted, without fear of being caught.

Like the text Anya had gotten last night.

Suddenly it all clicked into place. Zolo had seemed so weird the night before—he had been dying to find Anya. But then, once she was found—with Vance—he hadn't been relieved. He had been angry.

The threatening text had come just minutes after he had found out about their date.

"Oh, I just—I—I got it when my smartphone died," Zolo explained, getting to his feet. "I just needed something cheap, you know, and fast."

But I cut him off. There was nothing Zolo

could say to convince me this phone was just a convenient replacement. The only way to prove that it *wasn't* was to spend some quality time looking through the sent messages and phone calls.

"Sure, dude," I said. "Hey, listen, I just remembered I need to make a private call and I left my phone at the hotel. Okay if I borrow yours?"

Before Zolo could answer, I stepped out of the trailer, closed the door behind me, and started scrolling through the phone's history. I went right to sent texts.

SENT TO: ANYA

YOU MADE A BIG MISTAKE TONIGHT. AT THE BIG APPLE AWARDS, YOU'LL BE WITH VANCE FOR THE LAST TIME!

I swallowed hard. *Zolo!* He had sent the threatening text after all! Could he be the culprit behind everything?

Whirling around, I slammed open the metal door and burst in. "Hey, you—"

But I was too late. All I could see of our culprit was Zolo's leg as he disappeared through a rear window.

He was getting away!

Back on Track

"So then I told him, 'Listen, Zolo, I think you're being hasty about this,'" Vance went on, looking from Anya to me with a *Can you believe that?* expression. "Which was totally reasonable! I was just trying to get him to *attempt* the acting exercise. For someone who really wants to make the jump from commercials to features, he doesn't seem all that into *craft*, you know?"

Anya nodded, pressing an ice pack against Vance's cheek. We were sitting in front of his trailer, where Vance and Anya had decided to spend the break in filming. "We know, Vance," she said, looking at his jaw with concern. "We were all there, remember? You don't have to tell us what happened."

"That's right," I agreed, though it pained me a little to side with Vance against Zolo. "I don't know what got into him, but he was out of line."

"Totally," Anya agreed. Vance beamed at her, and then reached up to pull her face down to his, and . . .

I turned away. *Jeez.* It was like the seventh kiss in five minutes. I was happy that Vance and Anya were happy together, but . . . a bit much, anyone?

Suddenly I heard a commotion coming from the direction of Zolo's trailer, where he and Frank had disappeared just moments before. I looked up in time to see a Zolo-shaped blur zip toward us in a furious run, then slip by within inches of me, leaving a cool breeze in his wake. What the . . . ?

"Get him!" I suddenly heard Frank's voice calling. I looked up to see my very freaked-looking bro pointing in the direction where Zolo had just disappeared. "Joe, come on! Zolo sent the texts—and he's getting away!"

Zolo sent the texts? Wait . . . *Zolo* sent the texts? My mouth dropped open in surprise, but I trusted my brother enough to stop what I was doing and run. I could just make out Zolo's departing form as he leaped through the security gate.

"Don't let him through! Don't . . . *wait*!" Frank called from behind me.

But it was too late. Zolo was already off the set . . . and running through the wilds of Brooklyn.

I thundered after him, past security, as Frank caught up behind me. "Where'd he go?" he asked.

Without words, I pointed in the direction of Brooklyn's downtown. Frank and I didn't waste another second before powering off behind Zolo. He was about a block ahead of us now, moving incredibly fast considering he was wearing his alien-like Asp costume. The downtown area was bustling, but the crowds parted pretty fast when they saw a life-size alien barreling toward them. I realized that most of the passersby probably didn't know the *Deathstalker* movie was shooting nearby— making this a very strange sighting indeed.

We kept running after Zolo as he raced down a main shopping street and then darted through a little park. Frank and I were in good shape from all our ATAC training, but my lungs were still starting to burn by the time Zolo dashed back toward the street—and disappeared.

"Wait," Frank gasped, stumbling to a stop as we both looked at the spot where Zolo had been. "Where did he . . . ?"

Just then I noticed the stairway leading down into the sidewalk, bordered by a green metal railing, and I saw Zolo's head descending.

"There!" I pointed, scrambling into a run again. "The subway!"

We dashed through the park to the corner where the subway entrance lay—a different station from the one where the movie was filming—then pounded down the stairs, pushing astonished commuters out of the way.

"Sorry," we gasped, grabbing the railing and darting down in front of them. "Emergency. Sorry!"

Inside the station, Zolo ran up to the turnstile and struggled to boost himself over it.

"Watch which platform he goes for!" yelled Frank as we paused at the turnstile. "We don't want him to get away!"

Frank and I managed to launch ourselves over the turnstile, and I pointed Frank in the direction of the stairway Zolo had disappeared down. It was the downtown R train platform for trains heading farther into Brooklyn.

"Come on!" cried Frank, and we clambered down the stairs together.

An R train was just pulling into the station as Frank and I hit the platform. I spotted Zolo about halfway down the platform from us, turning to see if we were still behind him. As the train pulled to a stop and the doors opened, Zolo looked at me, his green eyes unreadable. He seemed to be debating what to do next. Then, just as the doors began closing, he darted into the train!

"Frank!" I cried, pointing, but my brother was way ahead of me. He grabbed me by the sleeve and dragged me into the nearest train car.

"Aah!" he yelped as the doors closed, catching his elbow.

"Stand clear of the closing doors, please," announced a jaded-sounding train operator. "Please do *not* hold the doors."

With that, he reopened the doors just wide enough for Frank to slide his arm all the way in. Then the doors slammed shut again. I could feel the brakes disengage as the train pulled out of the station, picking up speed.

"He's about three cars ahead," I told Frank. "Toward the front of the train."

Without wasting any time, Frank led the way through the crowded car to the front end, where a door led from our car out to a little ledge over the tracks and into the next car. NO PASSING, a sign over the door said.

"I think this constitutes an emergency," Frank said, grabbing the door handle and pushing it open. The door made an awful metallic shriek as he pushed it aside. We stepped onto the little ledge between cars, and I opened the door to the next car. The train was at its full speed now, and the noise it made as it rattled over the tracks was deafening.

The other car's door opened with a shriek, and Frank and I piled in. A couple of curious commuters looked up, but for the most part everyone seemed to be in their own little world—reading, sleeping, or staring off into space. We dashed down the aisle and passed through into the next car, and then the next. Soon we had gone through four cars, with no sign of Zolo.

"Do you think he got off somehow?" I asked, looking around the train car with a puzzled expression. "Is he in disguise?"

Frank snorted. "It would be pretty hard to be inconspicuous in his Asp costume," he pointed out. "And I don't think he had much warning that he'd be on the run—so I don't think he had time to pack an extra outfit."

I frowned. "Do you think he got off the train, then? Ran on while we were watching, then darted off through another door while we were distracted?"

Frank shook his head. "I don't think so," he said. "Let's keep going—to the first car."

We kept going, craning our necks to search each

car as we ran through, but there was still no sign of Zolo. When we were finally at the front of the train, we looked around desperately. But all we saw were sleepy commuters, absorbed in their books, e-readers, and papers. . . .

"Wait a minute," I said, pointing to a newspaper-reading passenger at the end of the car. From the waist up, he was hidden behind a copy of the *New York Times*—but from the waist down, he looked a little strange. Green tights led into a pair of space-worthy moon boots. Frank followed my eyes—then looked at me and nodded. "We found him," he said with satisfaction.

Zolo seemed to startle at Frank's voice, and soon a familiar green eye peeped over the top of the paper. Looking dismayed, if not exactly surprised, Zolo stumbled to his feet and slowly started walking—*toward* us.

"That's it," said Frank, a pleased smile blossoming on his face. "Give it up, Zolo. You know you're caught. All you have to do is tell us why—"

But as Zolo got closer, he suddenly sped up. He pushed Frank into me *hard*. We both tumbled toward a nearby bench, and onto a less-than-amused-looking elderly lady. As we struggled to right ourselves, Zolo darted past us—and back toward the door to the next car!

"Get him!" Frank yelled as we struggled to our feet. Within seconds, we were running after Zolo. He tore open the door to the next car and then, with a grim look in our direction, turned and peered up the side of the car. As Frank and I neared the door, Zolo suddenly swung his feet up and started climbing—*up the outside of the subway car!*

"Zolo!" Frank shouted. "What are you doing? You can't—"

But he already was. As we reached the passage between cars, I looked up and saw a crude ladder of metal braces leading up to the roof of the train car. Probably for maintenance or something— there was no *way* passengers were supposed to get up there. The train was still rocketing through a tunnel, and it didn't look like there was much clearance between the roof of the train car and the roof of the tunnel. In other words—going up there looked super dangerous.

I looked at Frank. He didn't say anything; he just nodded.

I started climbing the ladder.

The roof of the subway car was slick stainless steel—no foot grips, nothing to hang on to. And as I'd feared, there were only a few feet between the train roof and the roof of the tunnel. The train had to be going about thirty miles an hour at this point—fast enough to toss you off the roof, and definitely fast enough to do some serious damage if you were unlucky enough to fall off.

Zolo was crouched down on all fours on the middle of the car. Decked out in his alien costume, he looked like a space-age insect, holding on for dear life. He glared at me, but didn't move from his spot.

"Give it up, *Joe*," he said, his eyes steely. "You come any closer and one of us is going to get hurt."

I nodded. "And it'll probably be you, Zolo," I said, crawling up onto the roof, trying desperately to keep my balance as the train shimmied from side to side. "Look, there's something I have to tell you. I'm not really an extra, I'm—"

"Some kind of bodyguard-secret-agent-dude," Zolo supplied, his mouth curled into a sarcastic smirk. I looked up at him in surprise.

"Yeah," Zolo said with some satisfaction. "Way ahead of you. And I don't care."

Gulp. Well, there went negotiation strategy number one . . . and only.

"Okay," I said, shooting Zolo a grave look. "We'll do it your way."

Carefully, so carefully, I started crawling forward. The car was jiggling like crazy, and the roof was incredibly slippery. My knee slipped, and I panicked before bracing myself just in time to keep from tumbling to the tracks.

As I moved forward, Zolo scooted back—but I could tell it made him nervous. The train was still briskly moving along, and it jarred every few feet, sending the whole car lurching.

"Come on, Zolo," I heard Frank's voice urge behind me, where he'd climbed the ladder to the top. "You don't want to—"

Just then the car screeched as it rocketed into a curve. I felt the ground disappear beneath me and the cool *swish* of metal passing under my hands and legs.

I was falling!

I felt my heart leap into my chest as the tunnel twisted in my vision, remembering what Jimbo had said about the third rail—*how many volts of electricity?*

Enough to make sure this dingy subway tunnel would be the last thing I'd ever see, for sure.

Just then I felt a sharp pain as someone grabbed my leg—hard. I kept tumbling forward, but Frank had me. My body jerked against the train car as I managed to reach out my hands and brace myself. As suddenly as I'd started, I stopped falling, flopping against the moving car like a dying fish. After

Frank pulled me up, I took a deep breath. The putrid air of the New York subway tunnel felt like heaven in my lungs.

I'm alive.

I looked up just in time to see Zolo reach the far end of the car, grab something on the side (probably another ladder), and swing himself down. Then the train started braking again. I looked up and saw light flooding the tunnel—we were pulling into another station.

"Jay Street–MetroTech," the bored-sounding announcer stated. "DeKalb Avenue next."

Finally getting my wits about me, I scrambled to slide back to the ladder, then followed Frank down as fast as my legs would carry me. Darting through the door back into the train car, we got inside just in time to see Zolo running up the platform toward the exit—as the train doors closed, trapping us inside.

"Darn it," I said, and I'm embarrassed to admit that my voice came out a little squeaky. I may be a seasoned ATAC agent—but man, that was scary. "We lost him."

Frank sighed, throwing his arm around my shoulder. "But we kept you," he said, as we watched Zolo run out of the station through the scratched-up subway window. "That's what matters."

Guilty

"My dear colleagues, I'm sure you're pondering why I've called you all here," Jaan announced to what remained of the cast and crew a few hours later. We were all gathered outside Jaan's tiny trailer office. Confusion and concern showed on many people's faces; it was unusual for the director to call a meeting of the whole cast and crew on short notice.

I glanced at Joe. Of course, we knew why Jaan had brought everyone here. About an hour before, we'd met with him to go over everything we'd learned: that Zolo was behind the texts, that he'd run when I found out, and that he'd practically gotten my brother killed in a crazy subway chase.

Jaan had helped us convince hotel security to let us into Zolo's room, where the missing pieces of the puzzle were found. In a box under Zolo's bed, we'd found evidence connecting Zolo to the incidents: accelerant that could start fires, wire cutters that could cut through the wind tunnel's security net, and special electrician's tools that we suspected he'd used to electrify the microphone.

Zolo had done it all. The question was *why*.

"Many of you have gotten to know Frank and Joe," Jaan was saying, drawing my attention back to his speech. He gestured to the two of us, standing behind him. "But I wanted to share a secret with you all. Joe isn't merely a mild-mannered extra, and Frank was never truly Anya's boyfriend. Those were cover stories created to hide the truth: Frank and Joe are secret agents, and I hired them to protect Anya."

There were squeals of surprise throughout the crowd, and many people threw shocked looks at Anya, who hovered awkwardly behind us. Buzz, a cast member and former Broadway actor whom Joe and I had befriended, looked up at us and grinned. "Kick-butt, dude," he said with a laugh. "I should have known."

Vance looked up at us, then made a face like he'd tasted a sour lemon. "Well, they've done a *capital* job of protecting her so far, haven't they?" he asked, shaking his head.

I glanced at Joe with a *What the heck?* look. Vance was turning against us now?

Jaan raised an eyebrow. "My dear Vance, this is an incredibly complicated case," he said. "They've already removed three criminals from the set. Perhaps we can be a bit more understanding."

But Vance just frowned. "The only person I care about is Anya. It seems like the attacks and threats are still coming. Zolo is a maniac—he tried to kill me today—and he's still out there. These two let him get away. Maybe it's time to cut them loose and take this to the police."

Jaan shot an apologetic look at us before glancing at Stan, who was sitting in a director's chair with his arms crossed, watching the proceedings with a frown on his face. We knew the real reason Stan didn't want to bring this all to the police—he didn't want the bad publicity that would escalate when the public learned just how bad things on the *Deathstalker* set had gotten. But I also still believed—strongly—that Joe and I were the best people to solve this case. We just needed a little more time.

Stan cleared his throat. "Vance, keeping Anya safe is our number one concern too. Without her, we have no movie."

Vivian Van Houten, Harmony's agent, spoke up quietly. "I'm just concerned," she said, "that this clearly violent individual is still on the loose and meaning to do this production harm. Can you convince me—and these two young girls in the cast—that they're truly safe?" she asked, shooting a tender look at Harmony.

Jaan took a deep breath. "Vivian, I assure you, their safety is of the utmost importance to me. We're doubling our security on the set," he said. "No one will be allowed to enter who's not directly involved in the production, and who hasn't passed a background check. Frank and Joe are diligently searching for Zolo. We're on top of this, I promise."

He looked at Joe and me, gesturing for us to take over.

"The only thing we don't know," Joe added, "is why. We can't figure out what Zolo's motive was for wanting to hurt Anya."

He glanced over at Anya, who nodded shyly. "He was always so nice to me," she agreed softly. Earlier, it had taken some convincing for Anya to believe her yoga buddy had really been the one trying to hurt her all along.

Jaan nodded. "If anyone has any information that can assist the boys, or any inkling where Zolo might be, please talk to Frank and Joe. You can go now, everyone. But please be careful."

A quiet buzz of chatter took over as everyone stood up and started to disperse. Vance strode up to Anya, shooting a less-than-friendly look in our direction. "Come on, Sugarplum," he said in a voice like molasses. "I'll take you back to your trailer."

As Anya and Vance walked off, I turned to my brother. "Well, that's it," I said. "No more cover for us."

Joe nodded. "I guess it doesn't matter," he said, "since we know Zolo was behind everything. Now it's just a matter of finding him."

I nodded. "And figuring out *why*," I added. I turned back to the set, trying to imagine how Zolo might try to get back in, when suddenly Harmony's shiny blond head popped into my vision.

"Hi, Frank?" she said, looking pretty and nervous. "I . . . um—can I talk to you guys?"

"Of course," Joe cut in, smoothly moving in front of me like a metal shaving attracted to a pretty girl magnet. Was it me, or was he speaking in a deeper voice than normal? "What can we do for you?"

Harmony looked down at her hands, clearly uncomfortable. I noticed then that her agent,

Vivian, was lingering behind her, watching her client with concern.

"Tell them the truth, Harmony," she advised in a warm tone. "It will be better for everybody in the end."

Harmony nodded quickly, as though she was willing herself to believe it, then looked up at me. "I . . . Well, I know something about Zolo," she told me, biting her lip.

"You do?" asked Joe, still in his talking-to-a-pretty-girl voice. "Great. What can you tell us?"

Harmony took a breath. "He . . ." She paused, looking behind her at Vivian, who nodded supportively. "He had this huge crush on Anya. He used to talk to me about her, trying to get my advice on how to make her fall for him."

I looked at Joe. *A crush?* There was no denying it fit his behavior; seeming upset when her relationship with Vance was revealed, punching Vance, sending that threatening text. But how had we missed it?

Then I remembered . . . *Boyfriend Frank*. That was what Zolo had insisted on calling me while I was trying to pass myself off as Anya's beloved. He always said it a little weird, like he was bitter. And then I thought about Zolo's yoga dates with Anya, or the way he'd once saved her from a falling camera that we'd realized Anson, one of the crooks we'd already caught, had sent tumbling down on her.

I looked at Joe and could see him putting this together too.

"A crush isn't a motive to hurt someone," Joe said, putting my next thought into words before I could. (Brothers are good like that.) "It seems like if Zolo had a crush on Anya, he would want to protect her. Right?"

Harmony bit her lip again. "It wasn't . . . he was . . ."

Vivian came forward and put her hand on Harmony's shoulder. "Take your time, dear."

Harmony looked up at her agent and nodded, seeming to pull herself together. After a moment, she turned back to us, her eyes flashing their usual confidence. "I'm sorry," she said, looking from me to Joe. "I just always liked Zolo. I feel terrible turning him in. But . . . he was a little *strange* about his crush on Anya."

"How so?" I asked.

Harmony looked at me, her expression clear. "He didn't just want to date Anya. He wanted her all to himself. You know his mom is a movie star, right?"

"Okay . . . ," Joe said. "And?"

Harmony nodded. "Right. Well, he said her success and fame were really tough on his parents' marriage. His mom was constantly surrounded by handsome costars, and his father was constantly jealous. Zolo always said that he only had a few months to make Anya fall in love with him. After the movie was released and she got famous, he could never trust her to be faithful."

I glanced at Joe, nodding. "Weird," I agreed, "but that doesn't give him reason to attack her."

Harmony sighed. "Yeah. Well, up until today, I didn't think so either. In fact, I tried to *help* him get her attention." She shook her head. "I feel so stupid now. But that disposable cell phone you caught him with? The one you found in his backpack?"

I nodded. "Yeah?"

"I got it for him," Harmony said, looking down at the floor. Vivian leaned forward and patted her shoulder again. "I had this crazy idea that Zolo could pose as her secret admirer. I told him he could send her secret romantic texts from his disposable cell phone. Nothing scary—just 'You look hot today,' that kind of thing." She smiled. "The kind of compliments any girl loves to hear."

I glanced at Joe, confused. "Anya never told us about any secret admirer. . . ."

"It was our little secret," Harmony said, sighing.

"I don't think she thought they were dangerous—and neither did I. He never said anything threatening. Zolo was a funny-looking guy, you know. . . . But he wasn't the kind of guy Anya would fall for on her own. I thought if he could do something *really* romantic . . ." She shook her head. "With all this crazy stuff happening, I think they were the one bright spot in her day."

I frowned. "We'll have to ask Anya about this."

Harmony nodded slowly. "Ask her. Go ahead." She paused. "But what I'm afraid of is . . . I thought Zolo was such a sweet guy. I never really thought much about when he'd say he wished Anya would quit the movie."

"Hold on," said Joe. "He wanted her to quit?"

Harmony nodded. "He told me that was the only way they could be together for good. Otherwise, he was sure she would leave him for someone hotter or more successful when she got famous." She paused. "I thought he was just insecure. But . . ."

She reached into her pocket.

"Show them, dear," Vivian encouraged.

Biting her lip, Harmony pulled out a folded piece of white paper—a computer printout. She handed it to Joe, who immediately unfolded it.

"It's an e-mail," he observed.

Harmony nodded. "Zolo and I used to e-mail back and forth—it was our private way of talking about his crush on Anya." She looked at the paper. "A couple days ago, he sent me that. When I first got it, I thought Zolo was just being dramatic. But now . . ."

Joe held out the printout for us both to read.

To: Sweetharmony@fastmail.com
From: Aspguy@geeknet.com

Harm,

I really can't thank you enough for all the help you've given me on the Anya Project. But I have to admit it's frustrating that all the things that have happened haven't convinced her to give up the Deathstalker role. I know she could be a great actress, but I could give her a much better life. I would be totally devoted to her. We could get a little house in the Hollywood Hills, and I would take such good care of her. But none of that will ever happen if she gets famous and has her pick of any guy. Let's face it, I'm not the hottest hunk on the block or even this hotel.

I think I'm making progress, though. After that big shock I almost gave her, I showed her how to fall for me . . . in more ways than one. And I think I showed her how love can sting. That's why she needs me. If she's not convinced yet . . . there's a lot more where that came from.

Thanks again, Harm—
Zolo

My mouth dropped open. "The *big shock* I almost gave?"

Joe nodded, a look of disgust on his face. "The electrified mic at FanCon. I *showed her how to fall for me?*"

I groaned. "The vandalized security net on the wind tunnel stunt." My stomach turned. Zolo's e-mail mentioned it so casually—but the wind tunnel vandalism had led to an innocent stunt-woman's death.

"And love can *sting*," Joe added, looking down at the printout and then up at me.

"The scorpion in her purse," I said with a sigh. "Man, this is twisted."

Vivian spoke up. "When she first got the e-mail, Harmony was a bit confused by Zolo's words. She showed it to me, and we ultimately decided that they were innocent turns of phrase. But in light of what you boys just told us, well . . ." She pursed her lips, shaking her head gently at Harmony. "I know Harmony cares for Zolo, but better safe than sorry, I always say."

Joe looked thoughtful. "I still don't get it, though," he said. "He says he loves her—but all of these stunts were deadly. He could have *killed* her. Why would he want to hurt the one he loves?"

I shook my head. "Hold on, bro. He never says he wants to hurt her," I pointed out. "Maybe he just wanted to *scare* her. To convince her to give up the part and go live happily ever after in their bungalow or whatever."

Joe nodded but still looked perplexed. "It's a weird motive," he murmured.

"But Zolo is a weird guy," I said, looking back at Harmony and Vivian. "Right?"

Harmony nodded furiously. "*So* weird," she said. "But I mean, in an endearing way. I *thought*. Until just now."

Joe nodded again, more slowly. "Well, his reaction to finding out about Vance and Anya makes a lot more sense," he added.

"Right!" I agreed, realizing where he was going. "That's his worst fear—that she would choose someone better-looking and more successful than him."

Joe met my eyes, nodding more briskly. "And he

did run," he said. "When you found that phone, he knew he was caught."

"Nothing says *guilty* like running," I said.

But before we could discuss further, a sharp scream pierced the air.

"NO!"

It was a *familiar* scream. And it was coming from Anya's trailer.

All That Glitters

Frank and I took off running toward Anya's trailer. Inside, we found an unexpected scene: no Zolo, no wounded Anya. Just Vance and a defiant Anya facing off against Jaan and Stan.

"I won't do it," she insisted, shaking her head. "Absolutely not! With Zolo threatening me and running around somewhere out there? You have to be crazy!"

Jaan and Stan turned around and noticed my brother and me. Jaan looked a little sheepish. Stan just sighed, as if to say, *Another irritation I have to deal with*.

"Listen, sweetheart," Stan said, drawing a little closer to Anya. "I know it's scary. I know you've gone through a lot on this movie. I give you a lot of credit for sticking it out this long."

Anya glared at him. "I want to finish the movie!" she insisted, shaking her head angrily. "But I won't go to the Big Apple Awards! We don't even know why he's after me, but we know he's going to do something at the awards! No way!"

I cleared my throat. "Um, actually . . ."

All eyes turned to me.

"Actually what?" Stan asked abruptly. "You two finally turn up some information the rest of us are missing?"

Ouch. "Uh, yeah," I replied. I turned to Anya. "Listen, it looks like Zolo had kind of a huge crush on you."

Anya looked stunned. *"Zolo?"* she asked.

Frank nodded. "Yup, Zolo. And listen, we need to ask you—have you been getting any secret admirer kind of texts?" He cleared his throat, obviously embarrassed. "'You look hot,' that kind of thing?"

A faint blush crept across Anya's cheeks. "I mean, I . . ." She paused, looking at Vance. "Yeah. I got some very sweet anonymous texts. It was kind of a relief from all the *nasty* anonymous ones I was getting." She let out an awkward chuckle, then shook her head. "But I thought . . . when Vance told me how he felt about me . . . I thought . . ."

Vance furrowed his brow. "You thought they came from me, my love?"

Anya looked at him shyly. "Well—yeah." She turned back to Frank and me. "That's why I never mentioned them to you. They were this nice little thing, and I thought—mystery solved!"

I nodded. "That makes sense. But listen— Harmony just told us they actually came from *Zolo*," I explained.

"She got him a disposable cell phone," Frank added. "Harmony told us that she wanted to help him win your heart. But it seems his intentions were a little darker than she believed."

"What does that mean?" asked Vance.

"He wanted Anya to quit the Deathstalker role," I supplied. "He thought that was the only way they could be together—before she got famous and had her pick of, well . . ."

Vance puffed up a little. "Hollywood's elite," he finished. And it was clear from his expression that he thought he fit that description.

Everyone was quiet for a few moments, soaking up this new information. After a short silence, Stan spoke up.

"So it's decided," he said, putting on a bright expression. "You'll attend the Big Apple Awards."

Anya looked at him incredulously. "What? No!"

Stan held out his hands. "But from the sound of it, Zolo never had any intention of hurting you," he said, shrugging. "He only wanted to scare you. And he succeeded brilliantly."

Anya looked at him like he was crazy. "How many times have I *almost* been killed?" she asked. "How close does he have to come before we agree he's dangerous?"

Stan sighed. "Of course he's a threat, Anya. That's why we've doubled security. But listen . . ." He leaned forward, and lowered his voice to a gravelly rumble. "We *need* this."

Anya just watched him, quiet.

"This production has been running off the rails for a while now," Stan went on in a low tone. "We've managed to keep some of the problems out of the press, but we're way over budget, and now we have to recast Asp with someone who looks enough like Zolo Watson to pass for him." He paused, letting that sink in. "Do you know anyone like that?"

Anya was still quiet, but she shook her head. Zolo's unusual looks were what had gotten him the part as an alien in the first place.

"Anya," Stan went on, "I know you're frightened. But we'll ask them to triple security at the awards. And really, where would you be safer? Who would try to hurt you on live television?"

Anya opened her mouth like she was about to argue, but then bit her lip, looking thoughtful.

Stan glanced back at my brother and me. "*As I was saying*, I managed to get the cast a plum spot presenting the award for Best New Action Movie," he went on. "It will get people talking about the movie in a *good* way."

Anya looked torn, but Stan went on.

"And *you'll* look gorgeous," he added, pointing to Anya. "We got the up-and-coming designer Julia George to loan you an evening gown for the occasion. Not to mention thirty carats' worth of diamonds from the legendary jeweler Dan Worthington! Baby, you'll be on every best-dressed list this side of Paris!"

Stan grinned, but Anya didn't seem convinced. She looked at Vance. "I don't want to be on best-dressed lists," she said plaintively. "I want to live."

Stan shot Vance a look, and Vance turned to Anya with an earnest expression. "Sugarplum," he said, in that sugary tone we'd all gotten to know, "you know I won't let anything happen to you. I'd dive in front of a bullet to keep you safe."

I couldn't imagine self-centered Vance diving in front of so much as a ball of socks for anyone, but I bit my tongue. Maybe love really was changing him.

Anya took a deep breath. Suddenly she looked to me and Frank. "And you two will be there?" she asked, with a wan smile. "Right?"

"Of course," I said, glancing from Stan to Anya. "If you *really* want to do this."

Anya tugged on her lip for a moment, looking undecided. She looked from me to Frank to Vance, who nodded at her reassuringly.

"Okay," she said finally. "I guess you're right— Zolo never really wanted to hurt me. And I want to show the world I'm a professional." She paused, offering a shy smile to Stan. "Can I see the dress?"

Stan smiled—what looked like a warm, genuine smile. Seeing him smile made me realize how rarely it happened. "Sure thing, sweetheart," he said, moving to the door. "We'll send in the stylist."

Jaan and Stan left, and Vance followed—after giving Anya yet another uncomfortably long kiss and cooing in her ear for what seemed like an hour. Finally, Anya, Frank, and I were alone.

"Are you sure you want to do this?" I asked, plopping down on Anya's couch. "Go to the awards? You don't have to, no matter what Stan says."

Anya took a deep breath. "I want to," she affirmed. "I can't let the fear of Zolo keep me from doing what I want for the rest of my life. And if I want to be a serious actress, I need to get used to events like this."

Before we could reply, there was a knock on the door and Anya called, "Come in!"

In breezed a fortysomething blond woman, with deeply tanned skin and a perfectly made up face. "Hi, darling," she said, looking Anya up and down. "Oh, perfect! Look what a gorgeous little figure you have."

I glanced at Frank. "Uh . . . maybe we should go," he said.

"No, stay," Anya insisted, looking over at us a little uncertainly. "I could use an unbiased opinion about how I look in the dress."

Frank looked at me and coughed. I knew him well enough to know that that cough meant, *Gee, just what our extensive ATAC training prepared us for—fashion critiques*. I nodded to let him know I understood, but then shrugged. Anya could use extra reassurance right now—and it wasn't like we had any idea where to look for Zolo yet. All our preliminary inquiries—into his home, his favorite places, his relatives' houses—had turned up nothing.

With a flourish, the stylist—who introduced herself as Venice—disappeared with Anya into the room at the back of the trailer. In a few minutes, they both emerged, Anya in a long, drapey red gown.

Wow.

Anya was always a pretty girl, but in this dress, she looked downright gorgeous.

"How do I look?" she asked.

"Amazing," I answered honestly, while Frank just sat there with his jaw dropped. (He's always a little tongue-tied around pretty girls.) "You're going to be the prettiest girl at the awards—no doubt!"

Anya blushed, pink creeping into her creamy porcelain skin. "Oh, come on," she said, giggling. "I don't know about that. Huge movie stars will be there!"

Behind her, Venice grinned. "If I'm doing my job right, you'll outshine them all," she promised. "Now, for the pièce de résistance . . ."

She walked to the door and peeked out, calling to an unseen person. "Okay, bring it in."

As she came back in, a small, bespectacled bald man followed, holding a black leather briefcase.

"This is Harry from Dan Worthington," Venice said, and the man nodded amiably. "He's the guard sent to watch over the jewelry you'll be wearing—because that's just how valuable it is! Harry, open up and show us what you've got."

Harry placed the briefcase on the small dining table and opened it. Immediately, we were nearly blinded by the light reflecting off what looked like a mine's worth of diamonds.

As my eyes focused, I saw that the biggest piece—a necklace—was actually in the shape of a scorpion. "Dan's been experimenting with insect shapes this season," Venice announced, looking adoringly at the necklace. "When Stan contacted me about styling you for the awards, I knew you had to wear this."

Anya was staring into the briefcase with an open mouth. "Wow," she said. "Just . . . wow."

Venice nodded, unable to tear her eyes away from the briefcase's contents. "It's stunning," she agreed. "I can't imagine what it would feel like to wear it."

Anya perked up, looking from the necklace to Venice. "Would you like to try it on?" she asked.

Venice looked touched, but then quickly shook her head. "No, no. It wouldn't be . . ."

"Please," Anya insisted, gesturing toward the briefcase. "You chose such beautiful things for me. It's the least I can do."

Venice hesitated, but then looked back at the briefcase adoringly. "Well . . . all right," she agreed, chuckling nervously. "Just for a few seconds."

With wide eyes, she lifted the necklace—it looked heavy—and carefully clasped it around her neck.

As soon as she had gotten it on, though, her adoring expression changed—her jaw dropped, and her eyes widened with fear.

"Oh my gosh!" she cried, her hands scrambling to the clasp as her voice rose to a scream. "Get it off! *Get it off! It BURNS!*"

We all jumped toward her, and as we did I noticed a note we'd missed before tucked in the briefcase, in crude, messy handwriting.

OUT OF SIGHT, BUT NOT OUT OF MIND. I CAN ALWAYS GET TO YOU. AND NOW THAT I KNOW WE CAN NEVER BE TOGETHER, I'LL TAKE CARE OF YOU—FOREVER.

Dread

Two days later Joe and I got to the set bright and early, ready to watch Anya film her first scene of the day. Venice had been rushed to the hospital—it turned out the necklace had been treated with an acid that could quickly burn through flesh. Fortunately, she was okay. We got her to the hospital before any major harm could be done, but she was left with some bad burns. Still the question remained—how had Zolo gotten onto the set? Harry, the jewelry guard, had left the necklace unattended for only a few minutes while he used the restroom. He'd left it with a production assistant, who later admitted that she'd been distracted by a "wardrobe crisis" and hadn't been paying 100 percent attention to the briefcase. The note in the briefcase definitely seemed to implicate Zolo—"now that I know we can never be together." But how had he gotten on set without anybody noticing? Especially *after* the meeting where we revealed to everyone that he was the culprit?

I was pondering this mystery as Joe and I passed through the security gate—where the guard checked our documents like we were about to enter an FBI building—and walked onto the set. Filming today was taking place back in Central Park. The scenery would have been beautiful if everyone on set hadn't been too tense to appreciate it. Joe and I turned a corner and were heading toward the actors' trailers when I saw him.

Short. Thin. Dark skin. Long limbs.

Zolo!

"Hey!" I shouted, rocketing toward him before I could point him out to my brother. Zolo looked stunned, as I grabbed him roughly by the shoulder and put him in a headlock. "You should know better than to show your face around here after what you've pulled! You're going to go away for a long time!"

Zolo was quiet for a second, clearly taken off guard. "Hey, mon," he said—in a thick Jamaican accent. "I don't know who you tink I am."

Huh? His voice didn't sound like Zolo's. I looked down at him and suddenly realized that his eyes were brown—not the stunning green of Zolo's. And come to think of it, he was a little taller than Zolo.

Startled, I threw him out of the headlock. "Who are *you*?" I asked.

But just then Joe came up behind me and tapped me on the shoulder. "Um, bro," he said, gesturing to the path around us. "Look around."

I did what he said. And sure enough, clustered around Jaan's trailer were a bunch of Zolo look-alikes. From a distance, they all looked like our disgraced friend, but up close, they were different. One had a slightly lighter skin tone. One had longer hair. One had a mole on his chin. On closer inspection, one had to be at least thirty years old.

"What the . . . ?" I muttered.

"Come on," said Joe, taking me by the shoulder. "Let's check in with Jaan."

The security guard posted outside Jaan's trailer let us in. "They're holding auditions," he told us.

Inside, one of the Almost Zolos stood in front of Jaan and Stan, holding a script.

"You know what that means, Asp," Stan was saying, his gravelly voice completely unsuited for the role of Deathstalker. "We need to . . ."

"JUMP!" the Zolo-alike shouted, leaping about

four feet into the air. "INTO! ACTION!"

As he landed on the floor, the Zolo look-alike made a few quick karate mòves, looking around him suspiciously.

Stan groaned and pulled his script over his eyes. Jaan sighed and looked apologetically at the wannabe actor. "Thank you, kind sir, but I think we've seen enough."

As the actor thanked them and headed out, Joe and I moved farther into the trailer. "Uh . . . auditioning to replace Zolo?" I asked.

Jaan nodded. "Indeed. And sadly . . ."

Stan groaned and finished, "It's a nightmare. This is the hardest part to recast. You guys knew Zolo—he was a unique guy."

Jaan nodded again. "We've quietly put out a call to every agent in Hollywood and New York, even modeling agencies. But we can't find anyone who looks like Zolo *and* even *remotely* has the acting chops to take over."

Stan groaned again. "We're going to end up shooting a mannequin in a wig, just to get this movie finished. And it's going to cost millions." He rubbed his temples. "Just what I need to deal with, on top of everything else."

Jaan glanced at the door. "How many others are out there?" he asked.

I shrugged. "About ten or fifteen?"

"And are there any serious actors out there?" Jaan asked, looking hopeful. "The next Marlon Brando, perhaps, just waiting to be discovered?"

I looked at Joe. Obviously, there was no way we could tell that just by looking at the guys. But Jaan looked so desperate, I tried to paste on a hopeful look. "Um . . . maybe?"

Stan groaned and stood. "That's it," he said. "I'm taking five. Boys, why don't you tend to our leading lady? She's still acting a little nervous."

A little nervous. Well, yeah. Almost putting on a flesh-eating necklace will do that to you. But Stan seemed to have completely distanced himself from reality; all he cared about was finishing the film to "be done with it." And amazingly, he was still insisting that the cast attend the Big Apple Awards in two days. He was sure the publicity would somehow "save the movie."

Joe and I agreed to check in on Anya and headed over to her trailer, where she was getting made up for a big romantic scene with Vance. Actually, Vance had been her saving grace over the last couple of days. He still insisted that he could keep her safe, would stop a bullet for her, etc. As unbelievable as it seemed to the rest of us, it seemed to make Anya feel better.

When we walked into Anya's trailer, she looked relieved. "Hey, guys," she said. "See anything . . . unusual . . . out there?" She looked from Joe to me, biting her lip.

I looked at my brother, and I could tell we were both thinking about the army of Zolos. Fortunately, they were clustered around Jaan's trailer—far from where the scene was being shot. We hoped it was unlikely that Anya would run into them.

"Nope," Joe said quickly. "Par for the course. Same old, same old."

As the makeup artist carefully drew a clean black line along the edge of Anya's eyelid, she glanced over at us. "Did I tell you?" she asked. "I've decided I'm not doing the Big Apple Awards after all."

Joe and I exchanged glances. This wasn't the first time Anya had decided this; she had decided about three times since the necklace attack that under no circumstances would she attend the Big Apple Awards. Vance always seemed to convince her it would be okay. Why he was so insistent that they go, we weren't sure—but we suspected it had something to do with pumping up his own career. Presenting an award at the Big Apple Awards would land the cast in a ton of magazines, especially so soon after news of Vance and Anya's romance broke.

"Okay," Joe said in a noncommittal tone. We both knew this decision would probably only last till the next time she saw Vance.

"It just doesn't feel right," Anya went on. "If Zolo was able to get on set, what's to stop him from getting into the theater? I understand why Stan wants us to go, but really, how important is this stupid movie? I mean, does it really matter if the bad press makes it into a flop?"

Already, she sounded less certain. The movie—and its ultimate success—obviously weighed heavily on Anya's mind. She'd been specifically cast to play Deathstalker because she looked *exactly* like the comic book character, so this was her big—and maybe her *only*—break. If Anya really wanted to make it in Hollywood, *Deathstalker*, the movie, had to be a hit.

"You should do what makes you comfortable," I said honestly. "Whatever you decide, Joe and I will do whatever we can to keep you safe."

Anya looked relieved. "Thanks," she said quietly. Already, I could see her turning the decision over in her mind. "Maybe . . ."

But before she could complete the sentence, her phone beeped. Anya glanced at it, then at us. "Can you get that?" she asked. "It's probably a text from Vance. He's been sending little romantic notes every few minutes." She laughed. "I guess he's bored in makeup."

I walked over to the counter where Anya had set her phone and picked it up. Glancing down, my blood chilled. I could tell immediately this was no text from Vance.

I STILL HAVE BIG PLANS FOR YOU AT THE BIG APPLE AWARDS, it read. IF YOU DON'T GO, I WON'T HURT YOU—I'LL HURT HIM.

JOE

9

Talk of the Town

"Oh my God, is that *Natalie*?" Harmony gasped as we stood backstage at Radio City Music Hall. "Everyone on the A list is here! I can't believe it!"

I looked at my brother and smiled. Harmony was a television star in her own right—this wasn't her first time being around celebrities. But even a totally jaded person like myself had to be impressed by the sheer wattage at the Big Apple Awards rehearsals. And even more amazing, all the stars were dressed down in jeans and sweaters, chatting amiably as they waited their turn to rehearse presenting their awards.

Being here, I had to admit that I could understand why Stan had been so insane about the cast attending. It was fair to say they were the only up-and-comers in the crowd; everyone else was a bona fide star. Just *being* in this company would bring *Deathstalker* some serious attention.

But I also knew that Anya was seriously scared—and with good reason. She hadn't gotten any more crazy texts since the day before, but that was plenty to have her good and rattled. Even though security at the awards was being tripled, Anya still felt like she had to attend to prevent Zolo from doing something terrible to Vance. He hated Vance; none of us doubted that he had the motive to do it. Even Stan had finally seemed to realize how serious this was and told her she didn't have to do anything she didn't feel comfortable with. After all, we had no idea what Zolo's "big plans" at the awards were—they could be deadly. But Anya insisted: If she skipped the awards and anything happened to her leading man—in real life as well as on-screen—she could never live with herself.

Now, though, Anya was staring amazedly at the two-time Oscar-winning actress who was gushing to her and Vance. "What a beautiful couple you make! When I saw you on the cover of *US Weekly*, I thought to myself, there's the next generation of movie stars. How wonderful that you found each other!"

I glanced at Buzz, who rolled his eyes. All afternoon, huge celebrities had been approaching Anya and Vance to offer their congratulations. Some of them acknowledged the rest of the cast, but not many.

Buzz turned to Harmony. "How long do you think this big romance will last?" he asked her. "A week? Two weeks?"

Harmony raised her hand to her mouth to stifle a giggle. "Come on. At least she's happy," she whispered.

"Yeah, for how long?" Buzz asked again, widening his eyes. "Seriously—how long has Vance's longest romance lasted? A couple months?"

Harmony shrugged. "Something like that."

"She's survived so much on this shoot," Buzz said. "I just hate to see her get hurt by *Vance*."

They both looked over at the couple. Vance was cradling Anya's head against his own, petting her like a puppy dog and every so often kissing her forehead.

Buzz made a face. "*Ew*," he said. "And for the record, I think she's gorgeous. But enough with the PDA already!"

"Okay, maybe it's a little over the top," Harmony agreed.

Buzz looked at her incredulously. "A *little*?" he asked. "He's literally going to smother her with kisses. I'm worried."

Harmony tilted her head. "Was he like that with Amy?" she asked. "I don't remember."

Buzz shook his head. "No way," he said. "I've never seen Vance act that into anybody—except himself."

Harmony giggled again. "Come on, Buzz, be nice. Maybe he's a really sensitive person."

Buzz shrugged. "Or maybe he's playing for the cameras."

Just then, an announcement called all the performers in "the Fabula number" to come backstage. Buzz jumped up.

"That's me," he said. "Wish me luck."

In addition to convincing producers to let his cast present a major award, Stan had also gotten Buzz a role as a dancer in one of the show's big production numbers. It didn't hurt that Buzz and the pop star performing the song, Fabula, were friends from when he'd appeared in the Broadway musical based on her life. Even in rehearsal form, the number was super elaborate. It involved cables, acrobatics, and Fabula being raised onto the stage in a huge statue shaped like the Big Apple Award.

As the number finished up, Vance glanced at his watch and then planted a big kiss on Anya. "Excuse me, darling," he said, stroking her cheek. "Nature calls." He disappeared through an exit into the lobby, and Frank and I walked over to Anya.

"Are you sure you want to do this?" Frank asked, looking concerned.

Anya looked up at him with steely determination. She looked like a different girl from the one who had wavered back and forth on whether she'd come to the awards. "I'm sure," she said. "The theater security knows about the threat to Vance, right?"

I nodded. "Headquarters called them as soon as we told them about the text yesterday," I said. "They're turning the theater upside down searching for anything unusual. And you can bet no one's getting in tomorrow night without a background check and some serious ID."

Anya nodded. "Then I'm sure. His safety is worth this to me."

Frank and I exchanged glances. "Okay," I said finally.

Just then, a harried production assistant came running over. "*Deathstalker* cast, take your places, please!" she called. "Your award is next!"

Harmony, Buzz, and Anya—who were presenting the award with Vance—moved over to the edge of the stage.

"Places! Places!" called another production assistant, checking her clipboard. Suddenly she looked down and gasped. "Where are your shoes?" she demanded of Anya, glaring.

"So much for the celebrity treatment," whispered Frank.

"My shoes?" asked Anya, looking sincerely confused.

"Your *shoes*," the PA repeated, tapping her clipboard. "All female presenters are asked to bring the shoes they'll be wearing to the ceremony to practice getting down the staircase." She pointed to the stage, where a narrow, slick stairway led down to the podium. "Does that look easy?"

Anya was flustered. "I—no. I just didn't know . . ." She turned around to look at Harmony, who, at some point before taking her place, had put on a pair of green spiky high heels. "You brought yours?" she asked, pouting at her friend.

Harmony shrugged apologetically. "Vivian made me," she replied.

Suddenly a familiar voice cut through the crowd backstage. "Excuse me! Excuse me!" We turned around, and Stan's assistant, Julie, ran forward, holding aloft a pair of sparkly red platform heels.

Relief washed over Anya's face as Julie pressed them into her hands. "Sorry, I got tied up talking to the choreographer. Stan wanted to make sure you had these."

"Thanks," Anya said, beaming, as she slipped out of her sneakers and into the heels. "But wait! Where's Vance?"

Harmony frowned. "I thought he went to the restroom."

Anya nodded. "I know. But he isn't back yet."

The PA who'd asked about the shoes looked at her watch and frowned. "There's no time. You guys will have to rehearse without him."

Anya looked scared. I knew she was picturing all kinds of horrible things that might have befallen Vance. "But—"

I stepped forward. "Frank and I will look for him," I promised. "We'll find him and send him out there. Don't worry."

Anya was torn. But right after I spoke, an announcer intoned, "Here to present our Best New Action Movie Award, the up-and-coming stars of *Deathstalker*: Anya Archer, Vance Bainbridge, Harmony Caldwell, and Buzz Byers!"

Harmony and Anya exchanged glances. Harmony reached out and quickly grabbed Anya's hand, giving it a squeeze. "Let's go." She stepped ahead of Anya, and Buzz followed. They walked out onstage and began to descend the staircase. Anya looked at Frank and me, and I gave her an encouraging nod.

"Go ahead," I said. "We'll find Vance."

Anya gave me a nervous smile, but then nodded and walked onto the stage.

She turned toward the scant audience and gave them a million-watt smile, beautiful even in her jeans and T-shirt. Then she walked up to the first step—and her right foot slipped out from under her.

I was able to see Anya's confident smile crumple into a look of shock and disbelief as she tumbled forward—and fell rapidly down the staircase!

The Real Reason

In the chaos that followed Anya's fall, Joe and I sprang onto the stage and ran down to her, leaning over her crumpled body with concern.

"Anya?" I cried. "Anya! Are you okay?"

Slowly, very slowly, Anya pulled herself out of the fetal position and rubbed her elbows. "I . . . think so?"

"Can you stand up?" asked Joe.

Cautiously, she pulled herself to stand. "I think so," she said. "My ankle feels a little funny, but . . ."

As she said this, a nurse who worked for the Big Apple Awards ran over, instructing Anya to move her wrists, elbows, and ankles. In short order, she pronounced Anya to have "a slight sprain." She said she'd probably be fine the next day, but they should take her to the hospital to be sure.

Anya nodded obediently. "My feet—it was just like they went flying on their own. I couldn't even . . ."

Working on a hunch, I leaned over and grabbed her foot.

"Give me your shoe," I instructed.

Looking a little confused, Anya lifted her foot and obeyed.

I ran my hand over the shoe's sole. *Just as I thought.*

It was coated with a slick, oily substance. "Someone greased your shoes," I told Anya quickly. "They wanted you to fall."

Anya's face fell immediately, as she seemed to grasp that she was still in danger—even if she did what Zolo's threats instructed. The fall was more embarrassing than anything else—leaving Anya able to attend the awards and take part in whatever Zolo had planned. And it seemed that humiliating her was just the beginning. Suddenly panic flashed in her eyes. "Vance!" she cried. "If Zolo is here— if Zolo got in—he could be doing something to Vance! Remember how crazy he was on the subway tracks. . . ."

I jumped up, looking at Joe. "I'll find him," I said shortly. "Joe will stay here and guard you."

Joe nodded, giving me a meaningful look—*Be careful*—and I took off to find Vance.

First I checked all the restrooms, since that was where Vance had said he was going. Lots of big stars—but no Vance. I looked around backstage but couldn't find him.

At this point, I was starting to worry. Security wasn't as intense as it would be at the actual awards, but with the number of celebrities inside the theater, it was still pretty tight. Had Zolo really gotten through? And if so—had he finished what he'd started by pushing Vance onto the tracks during their last scene?

I reminded myself that the most recent text had said he'd hurt Vance only if Anya didn't attend the awards, but that was cold comfort. Let's face it—anyone texting creepy threats, putting acid on necklaces, and greasing shoes isn't playing by the rules. "But you *said* . . ." doesn't hold a lot of weight with criminals.

I searched the lobby, the orchestra, and even the mezzanine and balcony levels. No sign of Vance— or anyone who could claim to have seen him. Now I was really freaking out. Who knew how far Zolo's beating would have gone if Joe and I hadn't stopped it? Clearly, he had no problem with causing harm to Vance Bainbridge.

Sighing, I stood in the lobby and glanced out the main doors. Could he be outside? Maybe he'd needed some fresh air? Maybe he needed to call his agent and couldn't get service inside the theater?

I darted outside, then circled the theater. On a side street, I spotted the limo that had brought the cast from the hotel to Radio City Music Hall. Maybe he had forgotten something in the limo? Maybe Zolo had cornered him out here, outside the heavy security of the awards?

I approached slowly, and was soon rewarded with the sound of voices coming from inside the limo. *Vance!*

He seemed to be sitting in the backseat. "I need to rehearse presenting my award . . . I should go!" He sounded tense, like he was trying to convince someone to let him out. I tried to peer through the tinted windows but couldn't make anything out. Without waiting a beat, I pounded on the door. "Whoever's inside there, open this door right now!"

There was silence for a few seconds—and then the door opened . . .

. . . revealing a sheepish-looking Vance, covered

in red lipstick and canoodling on the bench with one *Amy Alvaro!*

I stared at them in amazement. Hadn't Vance just been smooching all over Anya inside the theater? "What the . . . ?" I stammered.

Beneath the red lipstick, Vance was turning even redder. "Oh, Frank. I'm so embarrassed."

I glared at him. "Wait a minute—what's going on here? Are you two-timing on Anya with your ex?"

Vance put his head in his hands, sighing dramatically. "Not exactly," he said. "I mean not . . . like you think."

Amy uncurled herself from his lap, giving me a challenging look.

I was officially really confused.

"I'm so sorry, Frank," Vance said. "Especially since I know you and Anya had a *thing*."

Clearly Vance had forgotten that we had explained just days ago that Joe and I were actually secret agents, and I had never been Anya's boyfriend. I decided to let that go. I still had to figure this whole thing out.

"What do you mean, not like I think?" I demanded.

Vance looked from me to Amy. She nodded at him, as if to say, *Tell him*. He sighed and looked me in the eye.

"My romance with Anya is fake."

Fake? My mind whirred. I remembered our conversation with Dalton: *It seems like a career move to me*, he'd said.

"You mean . . . you don't have feelings for her?" I asked. "It was all for show?"

Vance cleared his throat and nodded, staring into his lap.

It made sense, in a way. Vance's love-struck behavior around Anya had always seemed a little—well—over the top. Which would make sense if he were acting. His acting style was not exactly subtle.

"Why did you do it, then? For your career?" I demanded. Then a horrible thought occurred to me. "Does *she* know it's fake?" My stomach dropped at the thought of Anya keeping yet *another* secret from Joe and me. How could we possibly keep her safe if she wouldn't tell us the whole truth?

But Vance was shaking his head. "No," he said. "I wanted to tell her the truth, but Stan didn't think she would go for it."

Stan? "What does Stan have to do with this?"

Vance sighed again. "About a week ago, Stan came to me and said we needed something positive to put in the press to counteract all the negative things that kept happening," he explained. "He thought it would be a great idea for Anya and me to start dating—in the press, anyway."

I frowned. "So you went to her and professed your love?" I asked, feeling a little disgusted. I might never have been Anya's real boyfriend, but still—the things this girl had gone through on this set!

Vance nodded. "More or less," he agreed. "Then I took her out to a lounge where Stan had planted a bunch of paparazzi. A bunch of PDA later, we were on the cover of every tabloid in town." Even though Vance seemed sincerely sorry, I still detected a note of satisfaction in his voice when he said that last part.

I shook my head. Hollywood! "I can't believe you let her think that you were really into her, when all you wanted was to get some press for the movie," I muttered. Then, figuring I had nothing to lose, I added, "I can't believe she was really into *you*."

Surprisingly, Vance didn't seem offended. He shrugged, seeming to accept that he and Anya weren't exactly a match made in heaven. "Honestly, I don't know if she's really that into me," he admitted. "This has been a scary time for her. I think she just likes knowing that someone is one hundred percent on her side."

I looked at Vance. That was by far the wisest thing I'd ever heard him say, after "Craft services is great!" "I hope you're right," I said bluntly. Then I slammed the door on him and went back inside the theater to tell Anya the truth.

"You *lied* to me," Anya said, her voice surprisingly calm given all she'd been through.

We were all—me, Joe, Jaan, Stan, and Anya—sitting in Anya's suite later that night. After all the revelations of the day, I'd expected Anya to be exhausted. But instead, she'd insisted on confronting Stan this evening.

Jaan held up his hands. "I want to make this clear, my brave leading lady. I tell you this because you need to trust me to work with me effectively—I wasn't aware of any of this."

Anya looked at Jaan and smiled briefly. "I believe you, Jaan," she said, shooting an icy look at Stan. "I know *you* wouldn't do something so manipulative."

"Look, sweetheart, I'm really sorry," Stan said, looking sincerely guilty. "The truth is, I didn't think it would go this far. I thought it would be one date, smoochie-smoochie for the cameras, you'd get in all the magazines, and then it would be over. I never thought . . ." He paused, seeming to choose his words. "I never thought Vance was your type!"

Anya smiled a little ruefully. "He's not, really," she admitted, folding her hands in her lap. "I guess . . . I guess I just liked having someone. He told me I was amazing and he would take care of me." She looked up at all of us. "It was something I needed to hear, with everything going on."

"Anya," Stan said, holding up his hand as if taking an oath, "I promise you: I will do everything I can to keep you safe from now on."

Anya looked at him. "I wish I believed you," she said, "but Zolo has gotten onto the set at least once, and he got into the theater today. I'm beginning to wonder if you really *can* keep me safe."

I looked at Joe, frowning. As much as I hated to admit it, Anya was right. Despite our best efforts, we *hadn't* prevented Zolo from getting to her.

"I'm not going to quit the movie," Anya continued, "because I don't think quitting would satisfy him anymore. Besides, I *want* to finish this movie. And I deserve it, after all I've been through."

Jaan nodded. "That's certainly true, Anya."

Anya looked at Stan. "But I'm *not* going to the Big Apple Awards tomorrow," she said challengingly. "It's too much of a risk. And I realized today that whether I go or don't go, it won't keep me—or anyone else—safe."

Stan struggled to hide it, but I could still see that he was disappointed. Still, he nodded. "Whatever feels right to you . . ."

Anya nodded. "That's what feels right to me," she said, getting to her feet. "That's all."

Jaan and Stan looked at each other awkwardly, then stood and nodded at Anya.

"Okay."

"Good night, Anya."

Anya just nodded again, and the two men walked over to the doorway and let themselves out. When the door closed behind them, Anya sighed.

"Do you want us to leave too?" I asked gently.

Anya looked up at me, smiled, and shook her head. "That's okay," she said. "That might have sounded harsh, guys. But I know you both have been trying really hard to protect me. And I know you didn't know about the whole *Vance* thing." Her mouth twisted distastefully.

Joe nodded. "We want to keep you safe, Anya."

Anya smiled again. "I know," she said. "And I appreciate it. If you guys weren't here, there's no way I'd feel safe finishing this movie!"

I glanced at Joe. "Are you sure—you want to

finish it?" I asked. Joe and I had talked about it earlier, and while it killed us both to admit it, things just kept getting more dangerous for Anya. We both felt like we were failing in our assignment here. We'd lost Zolo, and he seemed hell-bent on hurting the girl he said he loved. Maybe if Anya quit the movie, she *would* be safer!

Anya looked me in the eye. "I'm totally sure," she replied. "Look, people have been trying to manipulate me the whole time I've been on set. Some with stupid intentions"—she gestured toward where Stan had been sitting—"and some with really, really bad intentions. I'm not letting anyone manipulate me anymore. I'm finishing the movie because *I* want to."

Joe smiled. "You know, Anya—you seem a lot stronger than you were when we first met you."

Anya looked at him and grinned. "Thanks," she said. "Now you guys can go. Get some sleep."

We said good night and were heading toward the door when Anya's room phone started ringing. We paused, and Anya looked at us quizzically.

"That's odd," she said. "No one calls me on the hotel phone. . . ."

Joe and I exchanged glances. *Uh-oh.* "Let us hear it," he instructed as we all walked over to the phone.

Looking at us with fear in her eyes, Anya slowly picked up the receiver.

"Hello?"

"Anya." The voice on the other end of the line was seriously freaky—robotic, but deep and threatening. "You'd better attend those awards tomorrow night. If you don't, you might survive. But you'll never be able to live with yourself. Because the whole theater will be blown sky-high!"

Sharp Dressers

Things were pretty tense as we rode to the Big Apple Awards. Anya, looking like a million bucks (or more—literally—with all the diamonds she was wearing) just stared morosely into space. She didn't seem to notice the fans and paparazzi who swarmed around the red carpet entrance. Even Buzz, Harmony, and Vance seemed nervous. Bomb threats have a way of putting people on edge.

Anya had barely slept or eaten anything in almost twenty-four hours. I knew she just wanted to survive the night. Any ideas she'd had about enjoying herself or hobnobbing with the stars were long gone.

At least Stan had contacted the award organizers to get them to quadruple the security. Radio City Music Hall was now harder to get into than the White House. They hadn't even wanted to let Frank or me in, until Stan had called the organizers to plead our case. He seemed to have seen the light and realized how dangerous it was for Anya to attend the awards. He'd tried all day to convince her to stay at the hotel. But Anya was determined to attend; she thought it was the only way she could keep everyone safe.

As we arrived at Radio City Music Hall, the limo paused in front of the red carpet entrance to let out Harmony, Buzz, and Vance. Frank and I had convinced Anya not to walk the red carpet. After the first three actors got out, the limo pulled around the building and let off Anya, Frank, and me at an out-of-the-way back entrance. Once security checked us out, we were taken backstage to wait until the show began.

Anya perched stiffly on a couch, nibbling on her perfectly manicured nails and looking super nervous.

"Are you okay?" Frank asked, his concern clearly overcoming his awkwardness around pretty girls. "You don't have to do this, you know."

Anya looked up at him like she'd forgotten we

were there. She gave a rueful smile. "Oh, but I do," she insisted. "Look, Zolo may be crazy about a lot of things, but he got one thing right. I could never live with myself if everyone else got hurt because of me." Her face fell. "I should've quit this stupid movie the minute my trailer was set on fire."

I moved toward her, offering a nearby tissue box as her eyes started to tear. "Come on, Anya," I said encouragingly. "What's happening isn't your fault. You know that, right?"

She took a tissue, sniffled, and looked up at me. "It isn't?" she asked. "Look, I'm no actress. Maybe all the fans are right to be mad that I was cast. And I didn't tell you about the texts from Zolo, even after I knew you guys needed all the clues you could get." She sighed. "Maybe I brought this on myself."

"Don't be ridiculous, Anya," Frank said, standing up to move toward us. "You've done a great job in the role. You're a victim here, not the instigator."

"Right," I agreed. "If Zolo wants to hurt you, that's nobody's fault but his own. Don't blame yourself for some crazy guy's crazy actions."

She sniffled again, and tears brimmed in her eyes. "But I was so *nice* to him," she said, shaking her head. "All that time I acted like we were great friends, and he was trying to hurt me."

I frowned. "Don't blame yourself for being nice, Anya," I said. "Anyone would have done the same thing in your situation. Nobody knew how wacko Zolo really was—including Frank and me."

Frank nodded. "That's right."

As he spoke, the same harried-looking PA who'd insisted that Anya wear her shoes the day before poked her head into the dressing room. "Oh, Ms. Archer," she said, looking at Anya with concern. "Are you all right? How's your ankle?"

"Um, my ankle is fine," Anya replied. "Still a little tender, though. I had to wear flats tonight." She lifted up her dress and showed the PA the pair of sparkly ballet flats Venice had insisted on choosing from her hospital bed.

The PA nodded. "I'm glad to hear that. That you're feeling better, I mean." She smiled. "Listen, if you're ready, the show is about to begin. Security can escort you to your seats while the lights are down before the first number."

Anya looked at Frank and me and took a deep breath. "I guess this is it," she said anxiously.

"This is it," I agreed. "Listen, Anya—we'll do everything we can to keep you safe. You know that. We'll be sitting right next to you. Okay?"

Anya took a breath and nodded. "Okay." She got to her feet, picking up the hem of her dress (which had been altered to accommodate for the flats) so she wouldn't trip. "Let's get this over with."

If you could forget the fact that an unhinged admirer was likely getting ready to hurt Anya and potentially blow up Radio City Music Hall, the Big Apple Awards were actually pretty entertaining.

I'm not a big awards-show guy. But the Big Apple Awards seemed a little younger and more irreverent than the established awards shows. The host, a comedian, was really funny; the presenters made fun of themselves; there were lots of fun dance numbers; and the speeches were kept mercifully short.

Frank and I were sitting on one side of Anya, with Harmony and the rest of the cast on the other side. (Vance was smart enough to take the seat farthest from her.) A couple of times, Anya reached over for my hand and squeezed it. I knew better than to think there was any romantic meaning to it; the poor girl was just royally freaked out and needed some reassurance.

Every now and then, the host would make a joke about someone in the audience and the lights would go up while the cameramen scattered around the theater to search out the person and get a reaction shot. Each time, Anya bit her lip and her eyes darted tensely around the theater. I followed her gaze, knowing she was looking for Zolo, and worrying that he had gotten in somehow. But each time, our search revealed nothing unusual. The host would continue his joke, and the object of the joke would smile and laugh good-naturedly, or else shoot a jokey "mad" look at the stage. Then the lights would go back down and the show would continue.

When I checked my watch for the first time, I was stunned to see that an hour had gone by. The cast's award would be coming up soon. When I turned to look up the aisle, sure enough, a PA was tiptoeing down. She paused at our row and whispered loudly, "*Deathstalker* cast? We need you backstage."

We all stood and moved into the aisle, and the PA looked at Frank and me with concern. "Um, sorry. Cast only."

"Trust me," I said, striding after the cast as they headed up the aisle. "Security will let us through."

Once we all got cleared to go backstage, we had a few minutes to wait before the cast would be called out onstage to present the award. Anya was pacing and chewing on her fingernails. Her eyes darted between the stage and the entrances to the backstage area. I knew she was scared. She even lifted her shoes to glance underneath, moving her feet back and forth on the floor to make sure they hadn't been greased.

"Anya," Frank said gently, touching her shoulder. "It'll be okay."

She sighed. "I wish I believed you," she said quietly, her face tense.

"Come on, Anya," said Harmony, taking her friend's hand. "We'll all be out there with you."

"Right," Buzz agreed. "Nobody will get to you if we have anything to say about it."

Vance looked uncomfortable, but he nodded too. "We'll protect you, Anya," he said. "That's a promise."

Anya looked at her costars gratefully, but I could tell she still felt nervous. "Thanks, guys," she said, and sighed. "I just want this to be over."

One of the PAs came over and told the cast to arrange themselves in the correct order and get ready to go out. The host headed to the podium to introduce them. I glanced at Frank; I knew we were both hoping that nothing would happen.

"And from the upcoming film *Deathstalker*," the host intoned, "please welcome Deathstalker herself, Anya Archer, along with her costars Harmony Caldwell, Vance Bainbridge, and Buzz Byers!"

Anya cast one quick glance back at Frank and me, and we both nodded encouragingly. She pasted on a bright smile and followed her costars onto the stage. I think Frank and I were both a little on edge watching her descend the same stairs where she'd hurt herself the day before, but the entire cast made it without incident. They all surrounded the podium as the audience cheered enthusiastically.

"Anya!"

I jumped at the voice that rose over the cheers. It sounded like it was coming from backstage, and it sounded like . . . *Zolo!*

"Did you hear that?" I asked Frank.

He nodded, and I could see from the look in his eyes that it had rattled him as much as it had rattled me. "Yeah," he said. "You don't think . . . ?"

I looked out onto the stage. Anya's face was frozen in a tense smile, and I could see that she had heard the shout too.

"Action movies," Vance began, reading off the teleprompter, "make us all feel more alive. . . ."

The cast took turns reading their lines, each leaning into the podium to introduce one of the four action movie nominees. Then they announced the winner, a movie called *Apocalypse*, and stood back while the cast and crew came up on the stage. Anya looked incredibly relieved. As the producer of *Apocalypse* began his speech, I could see a PA across the stage gesturing for the cast to exit stage left.

"That's it," I said, turning to my brother. "They did it! Nothing happened."

Frank frowned. "Well, except for that weird shout that sounded like Zolo."

I shrugged. "Nobody tried anything, though," I said. "We can ask security to sweep the theater looking for him. You and I can start searching backstage right now. But maybe we were just being paranoid—maybe it was just a fan cheering for his favorite new actress."

A few minutes later, Frank and I had done a complete search of the backstage area and found nothing out of the ordinary. We spoke briefly to a security guard, asking him to keep searching the theater for Zolo, then headed back to the audience to be near Anya just as the cast was sitting back down in their seats.

"Did you see that?" Anya asked with a smile as we sat down. "I did it! Nothing happened!"

I smiled back. "Sure did," I said, electing not to bring up the Zolo-esque shout. I knew she'd heard it. But since nothing had happened, it seemed more than likely it was just a fluke. Some teenager in the balcony who happened to sound a lot like our least favorite actor . . .

We turned back to the show, and after about twenty minutes the security guard we'd spoken to came down the aisle and whispered something to Frank. Frank nodded, then turned to me.

"They haven't seen any sign of Zolo," he whispered to me. "None of the guards on the doors have seen any suspicious activity."

I nodded. "Sounds like it wasn't really him we heard, then."

Frank nodded back. "Sounds that way," he agreed, with a little smile.

After a few minutes, it was time for Buzz to head backstage for his performance with Fabula. Harmony rose with him. She looked at Anya.

"We're almost two hours into the show," she whispered. "The whole thing ends in fifteen minutes! Maybe we'll really get through this, Anya."

Anya smiled. "I'm starting to think so," she agreed. "Maybe Zolo's big plan failed."

Harmony smiled back. "I'm going to go get a soda from the lobby bar. Want anything?"

Anya shook her head, and Harmony and Buzz filed out. Within seconds of their leaving, a well-dressed man and woman came down the aisle and gently poked Frank.

"Excuse me," the man said with a smooth smile. "We're the seat-fillers for Harmony Caldwell and Buzz Byers. May we get by?"

Frank frowned, looking at me. "Seat-what?" he asked.

But what the man was saying jogged a memory for me. I'd seen a special once on the making of the Oscar telecast. (Aunt Trudy was watching it, okay? And I had just made a big bowl of popcorn. I had to eat it in front of *something*.) When a star gets up—to present or accept an award, to use the restroom, or to get a drink—a "seat-filler" is sent to sit in their seat. That way, when the audience is shown on television, the theater always looks full.

"Seat-fillers," I whispered back to Frank. "It's cool—I know what they are. Let them in."

Frank, Anya, and I all rose to let the seat-fillers squeeze past. There were two awards left before Buzz's big number. The last two awards would be after that, then we'd be done. I felt a warm sense of relief settle into my chest. Maybe Zolo wasn't the all-powerful baddie we'd feared he was. Maybe the insane security Stan had put in place had thwarted him.

I watched as the cast of the Best New Romantic Comedy winner, *Men Are Martians*, made their speeches and headed offstage. The lights began to dim for the Fabula number. I sat forward eagerly. I wouldn't admit this to many people—but man, I enjoy a big, splashy production number.

But just as the lights were completely going out, Frank leaped up beside me. "HEY! What do you think you're doing?" he shouted.

I jumped up and followed his gaze over to Harmony's seat-filler—who had risen from his seat. Frank and I watched, openmouthed, as he pulled a long dagger from inside his jacket and lunged at Anya!

FRANK

12

Showstopper

"*Noooooo!*" Anya's shrill scream split the air just as the first notes of Fabula's most recent hit, "Cuddle Me," came from the stage.

Joe and I both lunged at once, vaulting past Anya and knocking the seat-filler violently into the woman next to him—and then down to the floor. I grazed the blade of the knife, taking a nasty slice out of my right hand as I tried to find the handle and wrestle it away. But the guy held tight.

"Drop that knife!" Joe ordered, bringing his leg around to plant a foot on the guy's chest.

The guy didn't answer, but instead pulled hard on the knife and bucked like crazy to get out from under us. Joe replied by raising his foot again and kicked the guy in the head, knocking him totally unconscious. With the guy passed out, I noticed a piece of paper fluttering to the ground next to him. Around us, people were gasping, leaping from their seats, and watching the free show that was taking place in the *Death-stalker* row. But apparently word hadn't gotten backstage, because as I raised my head, I saw thirty dancers taking the stage in sparkly silver outfits.

As I turned back to the unconscious attacker, suddenly the audience erupted in screams. I startled; what was going on? Had everyone suddenly taken notice of the knife fight in the audience that was already over?

But the screams only intensified, and I heard murmurs of shock from people around us. "Oh my . . ." whimpered a starlet in front of us. "That can't be . . . it can't . . ."

I stood up and looked at the stage.

And my heart stopped.

Because there onstage, beside the Big Apple Award statue where Fabula was supposed to make her entrance, was Zolo.

Or I should say, *Zolo's body*.

Because from the bloody stab wounds that covered

him, it was clear he'd been stabbed numerous times and was very much dead.

My mouth dropped open. "I can't—what the . . ."

Holding the guy under his feet, Joe stood to join me. "What are you . . . ?"

Then he saw it. His eyes grew to the size of dinner plates. "Oh my . . ."

"Exactly," I agreed.

Next to me, Anya was looking from the stage to the man under Joe's foot and back again. Tears filled her eyes, and her voice held an edge of hysteria. "What's going on?" she asked. "I thought—if Zolo is . . ."

I looked at Joe, gesturing to our unconscious friend. "If someone killed Zolo, then who is this guy?"

We looked at each other for a long moment, and then Joe looked down at the floor. I followed his gaze: The piece of paper that I'd seen fall out from inside the guy's jacket lay beside him. Joe looked at me, then reached down and picked it up. It was a folded-up piece of printer paper.

"Oh man," I murmured as Joe unfolded it.

A glamour shot of Anya, clearly printed off her website, stared back at us. At the bottom, girly handwriting spelled out:

ANYA ARCHER
Seat 18F
Make It Quick and Quiet!
Wait for Harmony's Signal

"Was he . . . a hired assassin?" I whispered, staring at the photo.

Joe looked at me. "Wait for Harmony's . . ."

My eyes widened. *"Harmony!"* I cried, thinking back to her "signal." "She got out of her seat to let this guy sit down."

Joe nodded. "We never suspected her, because she and Anya were such good friends. Could she be behind all the unsolved incidents?" he asked, his eyes bright. "But what about the text that we know Zolo sent, the one about being with Vance for the last time?"

I could feel adrenaline running through my veins—we were so close! "She could have planted the accelerant and everything in Zolo's hotel room," I added, remembering. "She wasn't shooting that day—she was back at the hotel."

"There's still the e-mail from Zolo hinting that he did everything," Joe said, shooting a meaningful look at Anya.

As we spoke, a security guard appeared in the

aisle. "What's going on here?" he demanded gruffly, looking from the stage down to Joe, the assassin, and me. From the chaos I could hear all around us, I knew that the security staff had to be *quite* overwhelmed at the moment.

I didn't miss a beat. "This dude tried to kill Anya," I explained, knowing that the staff had been briefed on the threats Anya faced. "And unfortunately, we kind of knocked him out before we could get any answers out of him. Now we need you to take him, because we have to go find Harmony Caldwell *immediately*."

"Harmony?" Anya asked, her face a mask of confusion. "Why would Harmony try to hurt me? She's my best friend!"

Sighing, I pulled Zolo's e-mail from my wallet, where I'd been carrying it since Harmony had passed it to us. "Does this look familiar?" I asked.

Anya unfolded the printed e-mail and scanned it, her eyes widening. "Oh my . . ." Her face fell. "This doesn't sound like the Zolo I know at all," she said. "In fact, that's not even his correct e-mail address. Where did you get this?"

I looked at Joe.

"Harmony faked it," he said simply, shaking his head. "And we fell for it."

"Come on," I said, as we quickly dragged the

seat-filler assassin to his feet and shoved him at the security guard. "We have some searching to do."

"What if she's gone?" Joe asked as we ran through the lobby. We'd just checked with the bartender—sure enough, Harmony had *not* ordered a soda at the bar. Which meant she'd left the row for other reasons. For example, to allow a seat-filler to take her place and try to kill her supposed best friend.

"You mean if she left the theater?" I asked. "Come on—let's check the bathrooms."

We did a quick search of the restrooms (our presence in the already chaotic ladies' room was not terribly well-received) but came up with nothing. Moreover, none of the people we spoke to had even seen Harmony. It was like she'd disappeared into thin air.

"Maybe she left because she knew we'd figure it out," Joe suggested, as I gestured that we should head backstage. "She could be in a cab to the airport right now. What if we lost her?"

I shook my head. "We can't think about that now. Come on."

The theater was in such total madness that we were able to get backstage without anyone questioning us. The security staff seemed to be stretched pretty thin. We could see that they were trying to hold the freaked-out performers in the backstage area so the police could question them when they arrived. But between the craziness backstage and the mad stampede toward the exits that was taking place in the audience, they weren't having a lot of luck.

I didn't see Buzz anywhere. "Hey," I said to a random dancer who stood in the wings, wringing his hands. "Have you seen Harmony Caldwell?"

He looked at me like I was insane. "That girl from the teen soap opera?"

I nodded.

He frowned. "Come to think of it, I think I saw her heading toward the dressing rooms as we were getting ready to go on."

"Thanks."

I found Joe, who was also asking a dancer (a pretty girl, naturally) about Harmony. She, too, thought she'd seen the actress heading in the direction of the dressing rooms.

"Come on," I told my brother.

We headed back toward the dressing rooms, quickly darting into the first one, then the second. All the lights were on, but no one was inside. A third dressing room was locked, but the light seemed to be out, and we couldn't hear anyone inside.

Joe groaned. "I have a bad feeling," he said, gesturing down the hall. An emergency exit led off to the left—and the door was wide open. In fact, there was so much screaming and shouting in the theater that I hadn't even noticed that an alarm was going off. Had Harmony really gotten away?

Just then Joe frowned. "Do you hear that?" he asked, scrunching up his face.

"Hear what?" I asked. It couldn't be Zolo again—Zolo was never going to make another peep. But when I concentrated, actually, I did hear *something*. A muffled female voice—just barely audible over the alarm.

"Help me! Please! Help me!"

I looked at Joe and could see he realized it at the same moment I did: *Harmony!*

Help? Me? Joe mouthed, looking as confused as I felt. I looked around, trying to follow the sounds to their source. The dressing rooms? No. The exit? No.

Then I noticed a smaller door leading off the hallway, shut tight and painted the same color as the wall, making it blend right in. I moved closer with Joe right on my heels.

"Help me!" Harmony called from inside.

I grabbed the door; locked. But a lock is no match for an ATAC agent. Grabbing my penknife from my pocket, I inserted the end into the lock and carefully wiggled it back and forth just like we'd been trained. Within a few seconds, I heard a *click* and tried the knob again.

This time the door swung open to reveal a janitor's closet, containing one bedraggled-looking Harmony Caldwell. In fact, it took me a minute to notice, but her hands and feet were tied, and she'd managed to slip off a gag that had hastily been placed over her mouth.

"Thank God you're here!" she cried, looking from me to Joe. "She killed Zolo and she has Buzz! I never thought it would go this far! You have to help!"

The Truth

"**S**he?" I asked, mystified.

"Vivian!" Harmony cried.

Vivian?

Harmony sputtered, "She—she had this crazy plan to scare Anya out of the Deathstalker role and get me the part. I *never* thought she'd kill anyone!"

Frank looked as confused as I felt. "Wait a minute. You're saying that *Vivian* killed Zolo?" he asked.

"And tried to kill Anya?" I added incredulously.

"And started the fire in her trailer," Frank went on, "and electrified that mic, and cut the safety netting on the tunnel, and—"

"*Stop!*" Harmony yelled. "Listen, I'll explain

129

"everything. But right now you guys have to find her! She has Buzz, and I think she's going to hurt him! I saw her and Walt, a security guard she bribed to help her, dragging him up to the lighting booth! Please, you have to stop her. Now I know she's capable of anything."

Frank and I glanced at each other. It occurred to me at that moment that I hadn't actually seen Buzz performing in the Fabula number. In fact, I hadn't seen Buzz since he'd left his seat. Did Vivian really have him? Buzz had been nice to both of us, and I hated to think that he was in danger. "I'll go," said Frank. "Joe, you stay here and listen to what she has to say. I'll be back as soon as I can."

Frank took off in the direction of the lighting booth, and I turned back to Harmony. "All right," I said. "You've got some explaining to do. Anya thinks you're her best friend, you know."

Harmony's face fell. "I know," she said guiltily. "It just—it got out of control so fast!"

I tilted my head. "Why don't you start at the beginning?"

"All right." Harmony took a deep breath. "Vivian originally put me up for the part of Deathstalker—Anya's part. She thought I would be perfect for it. I could dye my hair, and I've had dance training.

All the fight scenes and acrobatics would be easy for me."

I nodded. "Okay."

"Well, obviously I didn't get it." Harmony's lips twisted into a doleful smile, but she quickly bit her lip. "Instead they decided to cast Anya. But Vivian was convinced she wouldn't last. Since she had no experience, Vivian thought the part would be too much for her. She convinced Jaan to cast me as Susie Q, so that when Anya quit, as she was sure she would, I would be right there, ready to fill the gap." She paused and frowned. "The only problem was, when we started filming, Anya had no trouble playing her part. She was great, actually."

"Okay," I said. "So Vivian wanted you to have the Deathstalker role, but Anya got it and she was great." I raised an eyebrow. "So far you haven't explained why we're sitting here in this janitor's closet and you just sent Frank off to save Buzz's life!"

She looked up at me, her eyes wide. "I know," she said. "After we'd been filming a week or two . . . Vivian got a little weird. She started saying that maybe Anya *wouldn't* quit the movie on her own. Maybe she needed a little . . . push."

Hmm. "A push like a fire in her trailer?" I asked. "A push like some scary texts?"

Harmony looked at the floor. "At first I didn't know what she meant. I thought maybe she'd have a long talk with Anya and try to convince her that the actor's life wasn't for her. It's not easy, you know," she said with a touch of sharpness in her tone. "Having to stay in shape, constantly being judged, living from audition to audition . . . and trying to support your family."

"You support your family?" I asked.

Harmony nodded. "Such as it is," she muttered. "My parents only check in with me once a month. They usually call right when the rent check is due."

I gave her a sympathetic look. "It sounds like you're under a lot of pressure to succeed."

She avoided my eyes. "I am. I know that's not an excuse for what happened to Anya. But since I've been acting, Vivian's been the one person who looks out for *me*. She makes sure I feel okay about everything, and that my career is moving in the right direction. She's like a grandmother to me." She paused, her eyes darkening. "Or she was."

"So what happened with the texts and the fire?" I prompted.

Harmony sighed. "When they happened, I tried to convince myself someone else was behind them. And then you guys came along, and you caught Myles, and then Anson and Big Bobby."

"Right," I agreed.

"I told myself that they had done everything—even though they only confessed to part of it. But then, the night you guys were looking for Anya, Vivian came to my room. She'd been getting more and more tense as the movie went on and Anya didn't quit. But this time she was *really* keyed up. Like she'd drunk seven cups of espresso or something. I'd never seen her like that." She looked up at me, her eyes pleading. "She told me that since none of her little 'pranks' had worked so far—that's what she called them, 'pranks'—we were going to have to up the ante. But first we had to find someone to take the blame."

My mouth dropped open as I realized who the scapegoat had been. "Zolo!" I cried. All this time we'd been thinking we were protecting Anya from him. Was he really just someone Vivian had set up?

She nodded. "I was being honest with you about the disposable cell phone, and the 'secret admirer' texts," she said. "The stupid thing is, I really do—did—like both Anya and Zolo. I thought they would make a cute couple, if he could just get her to notice him that way."

I frowned. "But you did fake that e-mail you gave us."

Harmony blushed, looking down at the floor

again. "Vivian did," she admitted. Then she looked up at me. "But there's a part of the story you're missing. Zolo was really, really mad when he found out about Anya and Vance. He even stormed into my room that night and accused me of keeping it from him. He thought I was just humoring him with the texts and the encouragement—'playing him for a fool,' he said."

"Okay," I said. "But how does that lead to Zolo running away from us—and then turning up dead today?"

Harmony winced. "Well, he *did* send that angry text to Anya after she went to the lounge with Vance," she explained. "He told me about it when he confronted me. He felt terrible—he was ranting about how this movie was making him into a crazy person. But he was also furious about Vance. For the first time, I saw a dark side to his personality." She stopped and swallowed. "But he wasn't responsible for all the things you think he did."

I nodded. "Okay. So the next day, Frank catches Zolo with the text on his phone—and he runs," I continued. "And nearly gets me killed, I might add."

Harmony nodded. "Zolo must have felt terrible about that, but he was probably freaked out that you caught him." She took a deep breath. "And while he was filming that scene with Vance, Vivian sent me to plant the evidence in his room."

I frowned. Could Vivian see the future? "How did she know Frank was going to figure out he sent the text?" I asked.

"She didn't," Harmony admitted, looking down. "I told her that he had sent it. If Frank hadn't caught him . . . I was going to tell Stan about it the next day." She bit her lip. "And then he would have someone search Zolo's room . . . and they would find the evidence I planted. Vivian would be off the hook."

I frowned. "I'm confused. You say you didn't know what Vivian was up to . . . but you told her that Zolo had sent that threatening text," I pointed out. "You gave her all the information she needed to frame him!"

I could see tears forming at the corners of Harmony's eyes. "I told you, I was afraid of her!" she insisted. "I didn't want to frame Zolo. I really didn't. But at that point I was afraid of what she'd do if I didn't help her find someone to take the blame."

"Okay," I said finally. "So what happened tonight?"

Harmony blinked and a tear rolled down the left side of her face. "Vivian told me to meet her downstairs, under the stage, just before Buzz's number began," she said. "I knew she was going to do something to Anya—to *scare* her, I thought." She paused, horror growing in her eyes. "But when I got downstairs, I walked in on her yelling at Zolo." She swallowed. "I don't know how he got into the theater, or why. He was saying something about keeping Anya safe—'I had to keep Anya safe!' he said. But she cut him off, shouting at him, 'You idiot, it was me all along!' I realized I was seeing something I shouldn't, so I hid behind some props. And then—" She paused, horror creeping over her features.

I tried to make my voice gentle. "And then? What happened to Zolo?"

She looked at me, her eyes wide with fear. "She—she killed him!"

I couldn't believe it. Sweet, elderly Vivian had murdered Zolo? "She killed Zolo? How?"

She shook her head, as though she didn't believe it herself. "She grabbed a Big Apple Award off a table nearby and stabbed him with the sharp end. She stabbed him over and over, until . . ."

Gulp. "Until he was dead," I supplied.

She nodded.

We were both quiet for a few seconds, letting that sink in.

"I wanted to scream," she said finally, in a low voice, "but I was so scared of what she'd do. This security guard came downstairs then. She called him Walt. She ordered him to carry Zolo's body over to the big statue of the award. She must be paying him to help her. I realized then, it was the same statue that they would raise onto the stage during Buzz's performance with Fabula. Fabula was supposed to be inside it. But instead, Vivian and Walt put Zolo's body inside." She blinked, and more tears fell. "They were talking about how they'd already gagged Fabula and locked her in her dressing room. Vivian said she'd paid off one of the PAs, too, to tell everyone she'd already loaded Fabula into the statue."

I nodded. "The same PA could have greased Anya's shoes," I worked out aloud. "And this whole time, they didn't know you were there watching?"

She sobbed, then nodded. "They wouldn't have seen me at all," she whispered, "but then Buzz . . ." She swallowed, trailing off.

"Buzz?" I prompted.

She blinked again, tears streaming down her face. "He came downstairs," she said. "I think he was getting ready for his performance. When he saw me, he hadn't seen Vivian and the guard yet. I didn't have time to warn him before he said, 'Hey, Harmony,' loud enough for them to hear."

"Then what happened?" I asked.

"Vivian kind of . . . lost it," Harmony said, fear in her eyes.

"Obviously," I replied. "I mean, she killed Zolo right in front of you."

"No," said Harmony, "I mean, when she turned around and realized I was listening. She must have realized what I'd seen, because she ran over to me, saying, 'Oh, honey, this was all part of my plan,' and 'Don't worry, you won't get in trouble.'" Harmony scoffed. "Can you imagine? I'd just watched her kill someone in cold blood, and she thinks I'm worried about getting in trouble? She wanted me to pretend I hadn't seen anything. To just go back upstairs, have a soda, and wait until Buzz's number was over."

I frowned. "What did you say?"

"I said *no*," Harmony replied, like the answer was obvious. "She's a murderer! I told her the truth—which was that I might have been okay with scaring Anya a little, and I might have gone along with some things I wish I hadn't, but I definitely was *not* okay with killing anyone!" She paused. "And she—this expression came over her face that really chilled me. Her eyes just went cold. It was like there was nobody behind them. She said, 'My baby won't help me.' She said it over and over again."

I nodded. "Then?"

"Walt grabbed me and Buzz," Harmony went on. "As he dragged us upstairs, the dance number must have started. Zolo's body was revealed, and everything went nuts! Nobody even noticed as Vivian tied me up and shoved me into this closet. But Vivian told Walt to drag Buzz up to the lighting booth."

She looked at me, wide-eyed. "I'm so scared for Buzz!" she cried. "I mean, now I know she's willing to kill. What will happen to him?"

I stared at her, considering. *What indeed?* Was she telling the truth, or just covering herself? We still didn't know how Zolo had entered the theater, or why. What had he believed he was protecting Anya from? Was it possible that he had realized Vivian was behind the crimes?

Either way, someone had killed him, and I had every reason to believe he'd been murdered by Vivian like Harmony said.

Which meant that my brother, and Buzz, were up above the stage with a murderer and her accomplice.

Against my better judgment, I shoved Harmony

back inside the closet, still in her restraints. "I'm sorry. But I have to go help Frank!"

"Hey!" Harmony cried as I closed the door on her again. But I was already racing toward the lighting booth, hoping that I would find Buzz—and my brother—alive!

Crazy for You

I dashed away from the janitor's closet where Harmony had been held and ran in what I thought was the direction of the lighting booth. The whole backstage area was still in chaos; the police hadn't arrived yet, and the security guards were still struggling to keep a shrinking number of dancers backstage. Nobody noticed as I stepped hesitantly onstage and looked up, noting that a ladder led from a private box on the left side of the audience up to the lighting booth.

I ran into the theater, now mostly empty, and found the stairs to the box that held the ladder. Once there—the box was thankfully empty—I took the ladder two rungs at a time. As I got closer, I could hear voices above.

"You have most unfortunate timing," I heard Vivian saying. Her voice was chilling—totally unlike the warm tones she took with Harmony. As my head cleared the booth, I could see that Vivian and Walt had dragged Buzz onto a catwalk covered with lights that extended high over the audience. Normally, the lighting crew would be working up here, lighting the stage—but I guessed that they had been scared off with everyone else when Anya was attacked and a dead body turned up during the last dance number.

"Too bad for you," Vivian went on. "Now you're just another expendable actor who knows too much!"

I paused, trying to take stock of the situation. I could see that the security guard was holding a gun fitted with a silencer and pointing it right at Buzz's chest. I shook my head, trying to make the crazy scene make sense. *Vivian?* Harmony's mild-mannered agent? Trying to kill Buzz?

But I didn't have time to try to understand. I only had time to stop it.

Pulling my feet under me, I launched myself out onto the catwalk. *"Stop!"*

Vivian, the guard, and Buzz all jumped, turning to find me. The security guard quickly aimed the gun at me and fired, but I managed to duck just in time to feel the bullet whiz by my head. The momentary distraction was all Buzz needed. While the guard and Vivian were concentrating on me, he managed to pull away from the guard's grasp and run to the other side of the catwalk. But the guard collected his wits and lunged after me, grabbing me in a headlock.

Now *I* was the one in danger.

Vivian glared at me. "I knew you and your brother were trouble," she growled. "Always hanging around Anya! But you didn't prevent me from getting to her, did you?"

I decided to use ATAC tactic number one: Keep the culprit talking. "What do you mean?" I asked. "What did you do to Anya?"

Vivian's face seemed to crumple, as sadness suddenly took over her features. "You don't understand," she said. "It was all for my baby, Harmony!"

"What was for your baby, Harmony?" I asked, letting my eyes wander—stupidly—to my feet and the ground below. Oh, boy. I felt my chest constrict. I normally wasn't afraid of heights, but this didn't look safe at all.

Vivian sniffled. "Now even my baby has turned

against me," she said, and I saw a tear trickle down the side of her face. She swiped at it angrily, fixing her eyes on me with a fierce look. "Everything I did, I did for her. I wanted the world for her, you know. Fame, fortune—and to finally be free of those money-grubbing parents of hers." She scowled. "They didn't know how to love her. All they knew how to do was take her paycheck."

She paused, staring out into space, until I prompted her. "You knew how to love her, though."

She looked back at me. "That's right," she agreed. "I was the parent she never had. And when I heard about the *Deathstalker* movie, I knew this would be my baby's big break." Her expression darkened. "But then they hired that *amateur*, Anya, to play Harmony's part."

I nodded. "So you tried to scare Anya, didn't you?" I asked, my mind filling in the gaps. "To get her to quit? A little fire in her trailer? An electrical accident at FanCon? A scorpion in her bag? Threatening texts? You thought if she left the movie, Harmony would get her part."

Vivian nodded. "No one was supposed to get really hurt," she said morosely. "But then . . ."

I raised an eyebrow. "She didn't quit?" I finished for her.

Vivian caught my eye and nodded. "She was more determined than I thought," she went on. "And every day that went by, I knew it would be harder for Harmony to take over her role. I had to up the ante."

Up the ante. I thought of Anya's stunt double plunging to her death off the side of the Empire State Building, and shivered. "So you tampered with the security net on the wind tunnel stunt," I supplied.

"Yes, but I didn't mean for that girl to die!" she insisted. "I hoped someone would find it before she got on. But when she died, I knew I couldn't turn back! I'd already risked too much. I had to get my baby that part!"

As Vivian's expression got more and more desperate, my stomach turned. Clearly the stunt-woman's death had sent her over the edge. Maybe she felt so guilty about causing an innocent woman to die that something snapped in her brain. Or maybe she'd been a little nuts all along.

Either way, I was finally sure we had our culprit.

"But what happened with Zolo?" I encouraged her.

Her mouth twisted into a smirk. "Zolo," she muttered. "Such a smart boy, wasn't he? But not too smart for me."

I nodded. *Crazytown!* "You set him up, getting Harmony to tell us about his crush on Anya," I suggested. "You mocked up that e-mail for her to give us. And you planted all the evidence in his room."

Vivian glared at me. "I may have mocked up that fake e-mail, but *Harmony* planted the evidence in his room for me," she corrected. "And Zolo wasn't so innocent! He sent her that threatening text the night she went out with Vance!"

So Zolo *had* sent that. "That was wrong of him," I agreed, "but he didn't hurt anybody. *You,* on the other hand . . . you greased Anya's shoes so she'd fall during rehearsal. And you put acid on the necklace she was going to wear to the awards."

She laughed, a laugh so chilling it made me wince. And she leaned in, close enough that I could smell the champagne on her breath.

"Those were so easy! He really did love her, you know," she said in that cold voice. "Zolo was going to confess his love for Anya here—tonight! When she presented the award—in front of everybody! That's what he meant in his text."

I remembered the text Zolo had actually sent: He'd mentioned that it would be Anya's last time with Vance. Was that what he'd meant all along? He hadn't wanted to hurt Anya—he'd just planned to tell her he loved her?

"He told Harmony all about it," Vivian went on. "He thought if he told her how he felt in public—in front of the cameras and a full live audience—she couldn't say no to him. Everyone would be rooting for him, and she'd have to give him a chance."

Sad, I thought. Had Zolo really believed that was the only way he could get Anya to love him back—using a little Hollywood peer pressure?

"When he ran from you," Vivian went on, "I knew he was humiliated that you knew he'd sent that text. But I also knew he wouldn't give up. He cared too much about Anya. Even when he was still on the set, he was trying to figure out who was behind the attacks at the same time you boys were." She paused. "I knew he wouldn't stop trying to find the culprit. And I needed him off my trail. So I went to the public library, opened an anonymous e-mail account, and forwarded him the same e-mail I had Harmony give you."

What? "The e-mail you faked?" I asked. "The one where Zolo took credit for all those attacks? Why would you send that to *Zolo*?"

She let out a crazy chuckle. "That's right," she agreed. "He knew he hadn't sent it. And yet here was this e-mail, supposedly sent by him to Harmony. He knew he wasn't guilty of those crimes, and certainly hadn't taken credit for them. So what was he to believe?"

I tried to put myself in Zolo's shoes. I'd been framed for a crime I didn't commit, against the girl I loved. Then I got this crazy e-mail. I knew I hadn't done the things it said, which meant . . . "Harmony," I breathed. "He would have thought Harmony faked the e-mail?"

Vivian smiled again, her eyes still cold. "That's right," she said. "I prefaced the e-mail with an anonymous note. I said I'd caught Harmony with this e-mail and believed she was planning to hurt Anya at the Big Apple Awards. If Zolo could sneak in, I said, we could work together to protect her. I said I couldn't reveal my identity till then; if he wanted to keep Anya safe, he would come to the awards and help me." She chuckled. "It was all a game. A lure. I needed him here for the awards; I would kill him and use his body as a distraction while my hired assassin killed Anya."

I gulped. *Whoa.* She was seriously bananas. "But by then you'd have committed two murders to get rid of Anya," I said. "Weren't you worried that you'd gone too far? That Harmony would be seen as an accomplice, and never have the success you want for her?"

Vivian shook her head. "No, no, no. Harmony

didn't know anything about the murders. She was protected."

Okay. "All right. So . . . what happened when Zolo showed up tonight?"

Vivian breathed in before she spoke. "Zolo had replied to my anonymously sent e-mail saying he would attend the awards. He'd done extensive research about how the show was put together, and he planned to hide in a delivery of set pieces that arrived this afternoon. I kept my eyes and ears out, and so did the people I hired to work for me. And sure enough, I heard him backstage—when my baby was presenting the award."

The Best New Action Movie Award, I realized. Joe and I had heard right—Zolo had called to Anya from backstage.

"He told me later that he was planning to rush onstage and tell her he loved her, and that Harmony was the culprit," Vivian went on. "He thought if he accused Harmony in public, Anya would be kept safe. But Walt and I grabbed him before he could do that. I told him that I was the one who'd sent the anonymous note, and I would help him. But only if he came downstairs with me."

I swallowed. *Poor Zolo.* I had a feeling I knew where this was going. But I still asked, "Then what happened?"

"*I stabbed him*," she went on, laughing again. "I told him he was a fool; that it was me all along, not Harmony. And then I grabbed an award off a table backstage and let him have it! It felt so good; I didn't even know what I was doing. A few minutes later, I found myself standing over his bloody body with the award in my hand." She grinned. "I knew his body would make the perfect distraction. With him gone for good, I didn't have to worry about him figuring out the true culprit."

My stomach churned. Gosh, poor Zolo—he'd had his quirks, sure, and maybe he hadn't been totally forthcoming with us, but he was a good guy. He hadn't deserved to die like that, at the hands of this insane woman. And all for a part in some comic book movie!

"What about the bomb threat?" I demanded. "Was there ever really a bomb?"

Vivian just smiled an evil smile. "Of course not," she replied with a chuckle. "You boys and Anya are so gullible! It was a threat to get her here to the awards so my hired assassin could kill her—nothing more."

Unbelievable! "What happened after you killed Zolo?"

Vivian's face fell. "My baby came downstairs to meet me," she said, "just like we'd planned, though she didn't realize her seat-filler would kill Anya. But . . ."

Her eyes seemed unfocused, and she grew quiet.

"But . . . ?" I prompted.

She looked at me, and the tears started again. "She came too early! She and that fool Buzz, who came down to get ready for his performance. And when she saw me kill Zolo, she turned on me!" she sobbed. "I asked her to keep it quiet, but she said no! She was going to turn me in! I knew she and that moron Buzz had to be stopped."

I took a deep breath. Well, that pretty much brought me up to speed. She'd shoved Harmony into the closet . . . and she and Walt had brought Buzz up here. And now here we were . . . high above Radio City Music Hall's stage.

And it looked like I was about to become theater history.

Vivian seemed to pull herself together. When I looked up at her, she was glaring at me again, that cold anger back in her eyes. "Now," she said, "I'm afraid you'll have to go. Since you know the truth."

I struggled against Walt, but he had me good. I tried to put on my most sympathetic face. "Wait . . . wait!" I insisted. "You know this has gone too far, right? It's too late to get Harmony the part now.

She won't play it. And if you kill me, that's one more murder on your head. Wouldn't it be better to turn yourself in—to say you're sorry and take your punishment?"

Vivian looked thoughtful.

"You'd get some prison time, but we'd speak up at your trial," I went on, "and I'm sure Harmony would too. We'd tell the judge you had good intentions, but got carried away. Maybe the judge would reduce your sentence. And then Harmony could come visit you. You wouldn't have to lose her."

Vivian stared into the air for a moment, her eyes going out of focus again. When she turned back to me a few seconds later, her eyes were cold and hard.

"I've already lost her," she growled. She gestured to Walt, who lifted the gun, and . . .

"Noooooooo!"

All at once, Walt and I were both vaulted forward by the force of someone crashing into us from behind. Walt's grip loosened, and I struggled to my feet, running to the end of the catwalk where Buzz had disappeared. I glanced behind me and saw my brother grappling with Walt. He had his hands on the gun and almost had it away from the guard. I turned, running faster now, and . . .

Yikes!

My right foot caught the side of the catwalk and slipped, sending me tumbling. I had the horrible sensation of falling through space, with nothing to catch me. But I managed to grab the railing with one hand, then pull myself up enough to grab it with the other one.

I looked back to Joe and the guard while holding on to the railing for dear life. Joe wore a lost expression. I realized all at once that Walt had somehow gotten the gun back. Maybe Joe had seen me slip and loosened his grip just for a second. In any case, as I watched, Walt grabbed Joe and pinned him in a headlock. Vivian let out another spine-chilling laugh as Walt lifted up the gun.

"You boys," said Vivian in a raspy voice that reminded me of snakes, "are going to get a *dramatic* ending!"

Walt leveled the gun at me first. I struggled to get my foot back onto the catwalk, but it was impossible. I swallowed and looked down the barrel of the gun.

I'm going to die. I'm really . . .

KLONK!

A loud sound from where Walt and Joe were standing pulled me back to reality. Out of nowhere, a huge can light rose behind Walt and suddenly clocked him on the head! He sank to the ground, unconscious. And behind the can light I spotted an incredibly focused-looking Buzz, frowning down at his victim!

Joe took a second to recover. "*Dude!*" he said finally. "Thanks doesn't cut it! But where did you even *get* that?" He gestured to the can light.

Buzz shrugged. "They usually have a few extra hanging around in the lighting booth," he explained. "And don't mention it—you guys saved *my* life, so it's the least I can do."

Joe reached down and took the gun from Walt's hands as I finally managed to swing my foot around to the catwalk and pull myself up. When I got back to my feet, Vivian was trapped between Joe, Buzz, and me. She looked from one of us to the other, her lower lip shaking. She looked seriously nuts.

"Vivian," I said, moving toward her very slowly. "Just stay calm. You're going to come with us. . . ."

On her other side, Joe began slowly advancing. Vivian panicked, looking from me to Joe and back again.

"It's okay," I said gently, moving closer. "It's all right, Vivian. We're not going to hurt you. . . ."

She looked at me with unreadable eyes. "Come with me," I said, as Joe and I got close enough to grab her. She met my eyes, and the light seemed to go out of hers. I reached out to take her by the shoulders. She sighed, and then—

BONK!

Pain rang through my skull as I fell back in shock—

She'd head-butted me!

As I grabbed the railing, trying to keep my balance as I recovered, Vivian scuttled past me. She was incredibly fast for a woman her age. Joe ran after her, pausing to glance at me.

"You okay, bro?"

"I'm fine," I replied, though my head was still ringing. "Get her!"

Vivian was almost to the end of the catwalk, but Joe sped up, almost losing his balance as he ran after her. With one hand, he grabbed the railing, and with the other, he grabbed Vivian's shoulder.

"Stop!" he cried, as she turned around.

As her eyes met Joe's, I caught my breath. There was nothing behind them. It was like whatever human force had once inhabited Vivian's body was gone.

She looked at him for a moment—and then, in one gut-wrenching moment, she lunged over the edge.

She didn't even try to grab the railing as she plummeted downward. Joe and I reached for her, but it was too late. Vivian's scream cut through the entire theater, making the hair on the back of my neck stand up.

The audience was all gone by now—everyone had run for the exits after Zolo's body was revealed. I heard the crash, but couldn't bring myself to look. Instead I looked at my brother, who stared down with a horrified expression, then pulled his eyes away.

The End . . .

The expressions on everyone's faces as we sat once more around Anya's sitting room, drinking hot chocolate and tea from room service, were grim.

"And then as we were moving toward her, she slipped and fell," Frank finished, his face full of regret. "And that's everything that happened tonight."

Anya, who had washed off her makeup and was sitting in jeans and a sweatshirt, sipping herbal tea, looked shaken. She was still reeling from the discovery that Zolo had died trying to protect her, and that her supposed best friend, Harmony, had helped Vivian try to hurt her on numerous occasions. She'd been relieved when we told her that the bomb threat was a total fabrication—but it wasn't much comfort after a monster of a night. The awards had ended in chaos, and news reports were full of stories with theories about what *really* happened. Still, we were keeping the truth quiet until the police could verify everything. Right now, they were questioning Harmony at the local precinct.

"So it was Vivian the whole time," Vance piped up, as though he was just putting it together.

"That's right," I said. "She thought Harmony should have the Deathstalker role, and she got a little . . . obsessed . . . about it."

Buzz shook his head. "I couldn't believe it," he said. "I mean, she actually tried to kill me and I still have trouble believing it. She was like Harmony's grandmother!"

Jaan nodded. "I think it will take us all awhile to accept the extraordinary events of the last few weeks," he said, stroking his chin thoughtfully.

Vance turned to Anya, who was sipping her tea pensively. "Listen, Anya," he said. "I really am sorry for lying to you this week, leading you on." He glanced at Stan. "It may have been something I was asked to do, but I realize now that I should have said no. I knew how much you'd been through on this shoot, and I only made it worse."

Anya looked at Vance, her blue eyes lighting up in pleasant surprise. "Thank you, Vance," she said, and I could hear the sincerity in her voice. Then she smiled. "We probably wouldn't have made such a great couple anyway."

Vance looked confused for a second, but then he smiled and laughed. "Fair enough," he agreed. "But I hope you do find that special someone."

I glanced over at Stan, who'd been silent through this whole exchange. He was staring off into space, his tea untouched before him. He looked truly uncomfortable—like he was sitting on a tack. After a moment, his eyes focused and he looked around the room, leaning forward. "Listen," he said. "Everyone, I have an announcement to make."

We all looked in his direction.

"I'm suspending production on *Deathstalker*, the movie," he said with a sigh, "effective immediately."

Vance sat up in his seat. "No, Stan!"

Meanwhile, I noticed that Anya and Buzz looked relieved—if not exactly surprised.

Stan held up his hand, "Listen. I've put a lot into this movie, and I know you all have too. Many of you have literally put your blood, sweat, and tears into this production." He paused, looking around at Jaan, Anya, Buzz, and Vance. "But I know when I'm beat. Zolo is, unfortunately, gone. I can't imagine Harmony will finish the movie. We're so far over budget, there's no way we can recoup that money. And after the public disaster at the awards tonight, no one will be able to watch this alien movie without thinking about a crazy murderer loose in a theater full of stars.

"Besides," Stan went on, his expression softening as he looked at Anya. "I know the personal toll this has taken on you. Anya, I'm so sorry for pushing you to do things you didn't feel safe doing. I'm sorry for manipulating you with the Vance thing, and making you feel like you weren't the right actress for the part. I realize all of that was unfair. I got so caught up in making a hit movie, I forgot about the human part of moviemaking."

Anya looked at him. She didn't look touched, exactly, but she nodded. "Thank you for your apology, Stan."

He gave her a tired smile. "You're a firecracker, kid. I know you'll be a star one way or another."

Anya laughed. "Maybe," she said, taking another sip of her tea. "Right now, I just want to go home. Maybe do some yoga. Relax."

We were all quiet for a minute. Finally Jaan stretched and stood up.

"Well, this has been quite the trying night," he said. "Personally, I'm fatigued. I'm going to return to my room." He looked at Frank and me. "Can I speak with you boys before I go?"

I glanced at my brother; we both nodded and got to our feet, following Jaan into the hallway. He turned to face us, sighing deeply.

"Thank you, gentlemen," he said, shaking his head. "I admit, this case was more all-encompassing and bizarre than I could have imagined, but you both were diligent and brave in protecting Anya. I truly appreciate that."

I nodded. "That's what ATAC is here for, sir."

He smiled. "And you can be sure I'll be telling your supervisor how impressed I was," he replied. "Now, I need to slumber. I'm too old for this excitement, that's for sure. Perhaps I should take this as a sign from the great beyond that I should return to my artistic indie films."

"If I might ask, Jaan," Frank said, "what will you do next?"

Jaan looked thoughtful. "I'm undecided," he admitted. "I think I require a long vacation to clear my head. I have friends who have a little hut in Bora Bora; perhaps I'll go there and meditate."

I glanced at Frank. "That sounds nice."

Jaan nodded. "You never know where your creative muse will lead you, boys," he said, clapping us both on the shoulder. "It's been my distinct pleasure to meet you. Perhaps fate will allow us to meet again."

"Perhaps," I agreed. But after all the insanity we'd been through on this set, I had a feeling my brother and I would be looking for less stressful assignments.

Like swimming through pools of live piranhas.

You know, something easy.

. . Or Is It?

"Who's that? Who's that? Is that one of the actors?"

Straightening his tux as he stepped out of the limo, Joe turned and tried to give the paparazzi who flanked the Hollywood club entrance what he was sure they wanted: unrestricted access to one Joe Hardy.

Unfortunately, the minute they realized he was *not* an actor—just a nobody in a tux—they all lost interest and turned to the next arriving limo.

"Who's that? Is it Scarlett? Is it Natalie?"

I turned to look at Joe and shrugged. "Such is the life of a secret agent," I whispered.

Joe sighed. "True that," he muttered. Around

us, flashbulbs popped and the photographers continued to shout. The red carpet was covered with stars of various wattage, and we were most definitely the least interesting to the paparazzi.

"We'll just have to take comfort in knowing that we were the inspiration for Moe and Max Power," I said with a sigh.

Okay, okay. Moe and Max Power were the secret agents in *Dying for a Part*—Jaan's liberal adaptation of everything that had happened during the making of *Deathstalker*. We'd just seen the premiere and . . . well . . . they weren't exactly dead ringers for my brother and me. For one, they were both blond. Moe had what the real Joe had informed me was the latest and hottest new hairstyle. The "style" just looked like a shiny mop to me. Also, in the movie, Max was a huge nerd, always spouting historical or scientific facts and babbling like an idiot when he was around girls. In contrast, Moe was a ladies' man and a daredevil, riding onto the set every day on a huge motorcycle. (Max took the bus.) When I pointed out the obvious liberties they'd taken with our characters to my brother, he'd just smiled and crossed his arms in front of his chest.

"Really?" he'd asked. "You think so, Frank?"

My only solace was that Max saved the day at the end, rescuing the imprisoned pop star by ripping off his shirt and swimming through a tank full of sharks to nab "Veronica" and put a stop to her crime spree. According to Jaan, it was too expensive to shoot at Radio City Music Hall, so they'd had to "finesse" the scene where we caught Vivian. Also, he'd said something about "sharks scoring very high right now with test audiences." I never expected to be the basis for the hero in an action movie, but I had to admit, it felt pretty good.

No sooner had Joe and I started to move to the club's entrance, than all the photographers started shouting over one another as the flashes sped up.

"*Anya!*" I heard one of the photographers call. "Sweetheart! Look right over here!"

"Who are you wearing?"

"Are you single?"

The paparazzi descended on a tall, dark-haired beauty as she stepped out of the limo that had pulled right behind ours. She moved her long hair back from her face and smiled—and I was struck again by how truly happy Anya looked these days. It had been almost a year since the *real* incidents on the set of the *Deathstalker* movie. And when Jaan offered her the chance to play herself in *Dying for the Part*, I was surprised to hear she'd agreed.

She'd been amazing in the film, though. Vulnerable, strong, sympathetic—everything you'd want in an action movie heroine. Jaan had even written her a scene where *she* finds out that "Vick" is faking his affections. (The real story "wasn't cinematic," according to Jaan.) To get back at him, she replaces his self-tanner with gold paint. The audience had howled with laughter, cheering her on.

After smiling for the cameras for a few seconds, Anya looked up and walked over to us with another big smile. "Hi, guys," she greeted us. "You two look very handsome."

I cleared my throat, straightening my tux again. "Ah . . . well . . ."

Joe smiled. "Thank you. Shall we go inside?" He offered his arm.

Anya nodded and took it. "We shall," she agreed.

Inside, the after-party was already in full swing. Celebrities I'd only seen in magazines strolled around, waving at Anya or running up to kiss her on both cheeks. "Darling, you were *amazing*," one tabloid favorite told her, waving her glass of champagne. "Prepare to be the toast of the town!"

Anya smiled demurely, then led Joe and me over to a table where Jaan sat with Buzz, Vance—and "Zip" and "Vick," from the movie. When Anya approached, they all stood up and cheered.

"My beautiful costar!" cried "Zip," who, I noticed, had been flirting with Anya all night. And if I wasn't mistaken, she'd flirted back. "How does it feel to be a bona-fide celebrity?"

Anya gave him a warm smile as we sat down in empty seats. "It feels amazing," she replied. "I feel really good about my work in this movie. I just hope it leads to other parts."

Jaan laughed. "Oh, darling, it *has* to," he replied. "Your performance is a revelation!"

I touched Anya's shoulder. "I hear . . . um . . . I mean I've read that . . . you're even getting award buzz."

"That's true," Jaan said. "The awards committees are buzzing!"

Anya laughed, turning to me with a dazzling smile. "I can enjoy my career, thanks to both of you," she said.

I blushed.

Joe smiled back. "Anytime, Anya. There's just one thing," he went on, frowning in a concerned way.

Anya leaned forward, a crease appearing between her eyebrows. This was the worried Anya I knew! "What is it?" she asked.

Joe looked serious for another beat, then broke into a grin. "If you end up winning a Big Apple Award," he joked, "you might want to skip that ceremony!"

FRANKLIN W. DIXON

THE HARDY BOYS

Undercover Brothers®

INVESTIGATE THESE TWO ADVENTUROUS MYSTERY TRILOGIES WITH AGENTS FRANK AND JOE HARDY!

#28 Galaxy X

#29 X-plosion

#31 Killer Mission

#32 Private Killer

#30 The X-Factor

#33 Killer Connections

From Aladdin
Published by Simon & Schuster

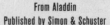

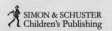